Credits

Author
John M. Stater

Developers
Bill Webb

Producers
Bill Webb and Charles A. Wright

Editor
Dawn Fischer

Layout and Graphic Design
Charles A. Wright

Front Cover Art
MKUltra Studios

Interior Art
Rowena Aitken

Cartography
Robert Altbauer

Playtesters
Frog God Games Staff

Special Thanks
Bill Webb would like to thank Bob Bledsaw and Bill Owen for inventing the original hex crawl — the standard in wilderness adventure and a lifetime of fun.

FROG GOD GAMES

TOUGH ADVENTURES FOR TOUGH PLAYERS

Table of Contents

Hex Crawl Chronicles

— The Shattered Empire —

By John M. Stater

For millennia the men of the north were pitted against one another in ceaseless battle, one city-state against another. In due time, the men of **Yal-Garok** gained the upper hand, dominating the minor city-states through arranged marriages and then striking at its greatest rivals militarily and forcing them to sue for peace. The rise of Yal-Garok ushered in the Age of Peace, allowing the clever, hard-working Northmen to focus their energies on building rather than destroying one another. Most of the country was brought under cultivation. Towns and cities flourished. Colonies were established in the eastern mountains, western prairie and, unsuccessfully, the icy woodlands of the far north.

The Age of Peace ended last winter, when Emperor Brodred passed into the Land of the Black Water, leaving his three daughters to squabble over the crown. And squabble they did. In short order, the youngest of the princesses, Petal, had her armies razing the city-state of the Princess Peahen and besieging the city-state of the Princess Pearl. Success on the battlefield, however, was not enough. To gain the throne, Petal needed to obtain the imperial regalia of her father – the scepter, orb and crown of the Empire. Naturally, her sisters also sought these items, sending agents throughout the land to seek them out.

This then, is the Shattered Empire, a land of marching armies, desperate refugees, highwaymen and bandits and encroaching humanoids from across the White River. A band of adventures might come into this land as seekers after lost treasures, common bandits or even mercenary captains seeking to join the winning side in the civil war.

The Shattered Empire is a hex-crawl, referring to the hex-shaped units that divide the map. Just as dungeon adventures take place on a gridded map, wilderness adventures can be conducted on a hex map, allowing players the freedom to decide where their characters roam and giving them the thrill of discovering the many places and people that have been placed on the map. This map represents a large area filled with numerous places to discover and explore, and can be used as a campaign area in its own right, or dropped into an existing campaign. Referees can place adventures they have purchased or devised on their own into empty hexes on the map.

Adventures in the Wilderness

The hexes on this map are 6 miles wide from one side to the other. In open country, adventurers should be able to see from one side of the hex to another. In wooded hexes, vision is much more restricted. Random encounters with monsters should be diced for each day and each night, with encounters occurring on the roll of 1-2 on 1d6. The exact monster (or monsters) encountered depends on the terrain through which the adventurers are traveling. Unlike dungeons, in which the monsters on the upper levels are usually less powerful than the monsters on deeper levels, wilderness encounters are quite variable in their challenge, and low level characters face death every time they step out of the confines of civilization. Well-traveled adventurers will discover, however, that settled lands are not as dangerous as the rugged wilderness.

The Imperial Regalia

The Imperial Regalia are the three ancient artifacts of the Northmen and their empire. Each of the objects was forged by one of the three great cities of the Empire and blessed by that city's priests. The first to bear these objects was Beroldern, King of Yal-Garok and founder of the Empire.

The *Orb of Yal-Kirith* is made of brownish marble and covered in a mesh of gold wire decorated liberally with citrines and rubies. When placed in a vessel of water, the orb turns that water into a scrying pool (treat as a *crystal ball*). When requesting a vision from the pool, an adventurer must roll 1d20 and compare it to his character's wisdom score. If the roll is higher than the adventurer's Wisdom, the pool shows the person what they want to be true rather than what is actually true. The *Orb* is hidden in the tower in hex 0418.

The *Scepter of Yal-Zanath* is a gold rod four feet long topped by a

Roll	Farmland	Highlands	Swamp	Wooded Hills
1	Ankheg (1d4)	Bandits (1d6 x8)	Catoblepas (1)	Black Bear (1d6 x4)
2	Bandits (1d6 x4)	Black Bear (1d6)	Carrion Fly (1)	Bugbears (1d6 x8)
3	Black Bear (1d6)	Bugbears (2d6)	Halfling (1d10 x10)	Centaurs (1d6 x4)
4	Giant Ant (2d6)	Centaur (1d4)	Goblins (1d10 x10)	Goblins (1d10 x20)
5	Giant Toad (1)	Goblins (1d6 x10)	Grey Ooze (1d6)	Hobgoblins (1d6 x30)
6	Goblins (1d6 x8)	Hill Giant (1)	Shambling Mound (1)	Men-At-Arms (1d6 x30)
7	Men-At-Arms (1d6 x4)	Men-At-Arms (1d6 x8)	Skeletons (1d8 x10)	Orcs (1d6 x30)
8	Ogre (1)	Ogres (1d6)	Stirge (1d8 x10)	Owlbear (2d6)
9	Wolves (2d6)	Wolves (1d6 x4)	Wight (1d6)	Wolves (1d6 x6)
10	Zombies (2d6)	Zombies (1d6 x4)	Zombies (1d6 x8)	Zombies (1d8 x10)

Note: For large bodies of humanoid troops, feel free to organize them into squadrons and companies using the army composition suggestions below.

platinum bear rampant with amethyst eyes. The length of the rod is studded with amethyst intaglios of past emperors and empresses. The scepter allows its wielder to use the following spells, each three times per day: *Hold person, cause fear* and *cure light wounds*. The scepter can also be wielded as a *+2 mace*. The *Scepter* is hidden in the nature temple in hex 3503.

The *Crown of Yal-Garok* is a band of gold adorned with silver spikes tipped with sapphire orbs. The wearer of the crown can command the obedience and fealty of creatures within 120 feet. Creatures totaling 300 Hit Dice can be ruled, but intelligent creatures are entitled to a saving throw to negate the effect. Ruled creatures obey the wielder as if she were their absolute sovereign. The crown can be used for 500 total minutes before crumbling to dust. This duration need not be continuous. The crown is in the possession of the angel Tzaqiel in hex 3822.

The Princesses Imperial

The Emperor Brodred was not only a fortunate man, but a fecund one. His empress Gurdolena gave him five surviving children, two sons and three daughters. His two sons, Brene and Beorwin, left the comfort of the Empire to adventure in the mysterious west. After they crossed the western border of the Empire they passed from the knowledge of men and some folk still pray for their return.

The three daughters of Brodred and Gurdolena are called Petal, Peahen and Pearl. Pearl was the eldest. Born holy, she grew up to sup with demons. Her blazon is a purple six-pointed star on a field of gold. Peahen was born plain and grew to be beautiful. The darling of the seven cities, her blazon is a peacock on a field of green. The youngest daughter was Petal, who was born pretty and grew up to be shrewd. Ignored by her sisters, it is said she had foreknowledge of her father's death. Certainly she moved the most swiftly to usurp his power and launch the elements of his army that were loyal to her against her sisters. Petal's emblem is a pink rose on a field of white.

The Armies

The armies of the Shattered Empire hex crawl are defined as being made up of squadrons of 10 warriors or companies of 20 warriors. Horsemen are organized into squadrons and foot soldiers into companies. Each squadron is made up of nine men-at-arms under the command of a sergeant-at-arms, while each company consists of 17 men-at-arms under the command of a captain and two sergeants-at-arms. There is a 1% chance that a sergeant-at-arms is actually a hero (i.e. a fighting-man of 3rd to 6th level). There is a 5% chance that a captain is actually a hero. Humanoid armies are organized using the same basic system, save their captains are called chieftains and their sergeants are sub-chiefs.

The precise elements of an army can be generated using the following tables:

Mounted Soldiers

Goblins are always mounted on wolves and orcs on giant boars. Among the savage humanoids, only hobgoblins have tamed the horse and even then rely on light, swift horses rather than heavy destriers.

Roll	Northmen	Hobgoblins
1	Hussars	Hussars
2	Hobelars	Hussars
3	Cataphracts	Hobelars
4	Knights	Hobelars

Hobelars are light horsemen who sometimes dismount before battle.

Hobelars wear leather armor and carry longsword and lance.

Hussars are mounted archers capable of firing their bows from horseback at a full gallop. Hussars wear leather armor and carry shortbows and longswords.

Cataphracts are heavy horsemen wearing chainmail hauberks and carrying light steel shields, lances and longswords.

Knights are the heaviest horsemen, usually drawn from the nobility. Knights wear plate armor and carry heavy shields, lances and longswords.

Foot Soldiers

Roll	Northmen	Goblins	Orcs	Hobgoblins
1	Militia	Archers	Archers	Archers
2-3	Archers	Archers	Archers	Light Foot
4-5	Light Foot	Light Foot	Light Foot	Light Foot
6	Longbowmen	Light Foot	Light Foot	Longbowmen
7	Heavy Foot	Heavy Foot	Heavy Foot	Heavy Foot
8	Special	Special	Special	Special

Militia consists of peasants rather than men-at-arms. A militia company numbers 40 men, each carrying light wooden shield, spear and possibly (50% chance) slings.

Light Footmen wear scale armor and carry shield, spear and short sword.

Heavy Footmen wear chainmail and carry polearm and short sword.

Archers wear leather armor and carry short bow, 20 arrows and hand axe.

Longbowmen wear scale armor and carry long bow, 20 arrows and short sword

Special troops might include **pikemen**, **war mammoths** with handlers, **berserkers** armed with battle axes or **scouts**. Scout companies are composed of 10 troops wearing leather armor and armed with daggers and short bows.
Gear Hide armor, battleaxe

Armies in the Field

At the start of any campaign in the Shattered Empire, there are three armies in the field, those of Petal, Pearl and Peahen.

The army of Petal is currently engaged in the siege of Yal-Kirith [3411], and thus encamped around that city. Petal's army consists of 10 squadrons of horse and 15 companies of foot, as well as siege engineers and their war engines.

Upon hearing the news of her father's death, the Princess Peahen split her army into three legions and sent them to secure the lesser city-states of Xom-Cahar [0208], Xom-Yeric [0803] and Xom-Iforn [1607]. Leaving only a small garrison to defend Yal-Zanath [1007], that city-state was swiftly taken and razed to the ground by the army of Petal. The three legions of Peahen's army remain in the field. The Legion I consists of 2 squadrons of horse and 3 companies of foot and is headquartered at Xom-Yeric awaiting its mistress. Legion II consists of 2 squadrons of horse and 4 companies of foot and begins the campaign at Xom-Cahar. Legion II will begin moving towards Xom-Yeric, managing to cover one hex on a roll of 1-2 on 1d6 made each round. Legion III is headquartered at Xom-Iforn and consists of 1 squadron of horse and 2 companies of foot.

Princess Pearl was slow to act upon learning of her father's demise.

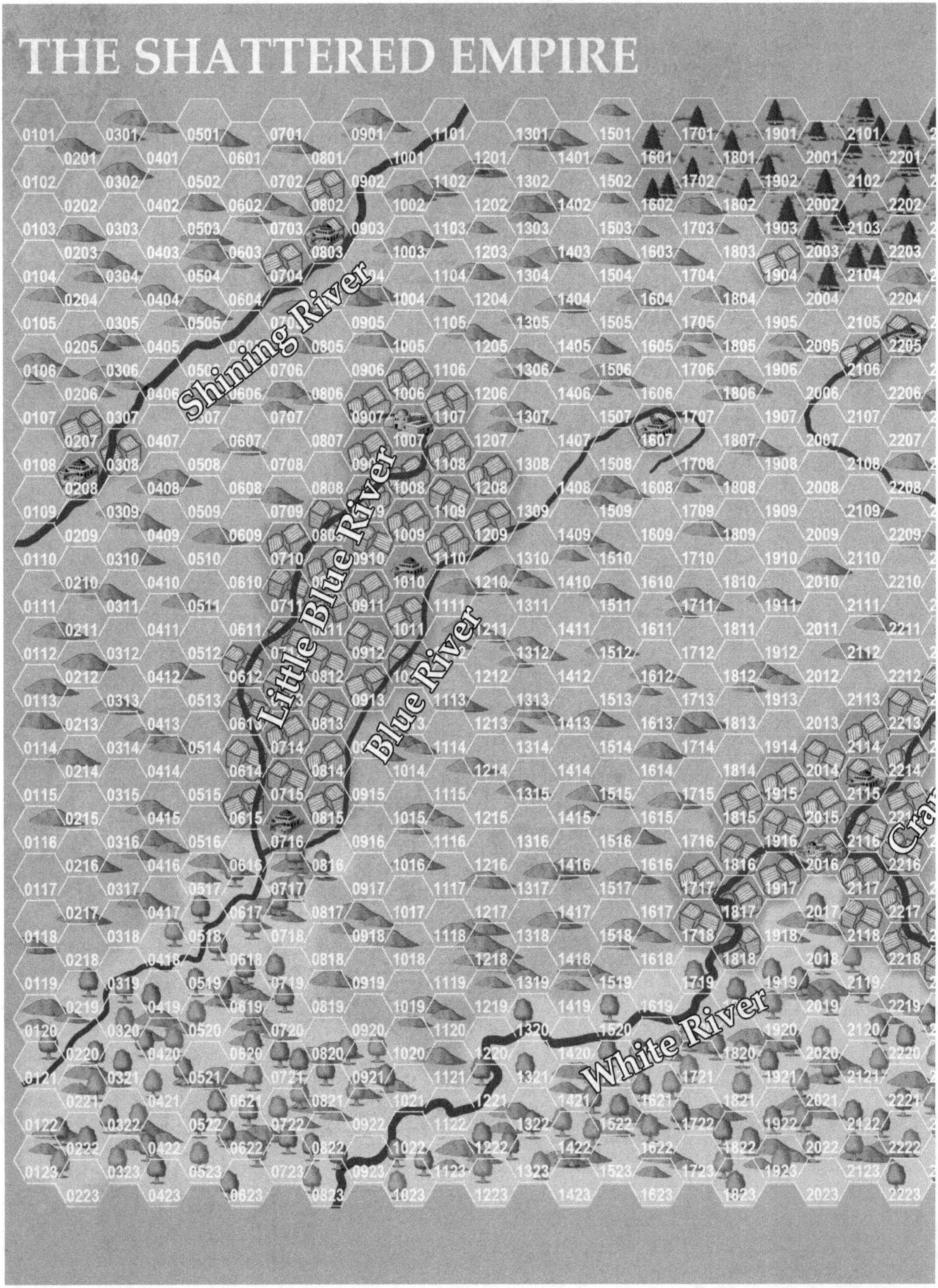

THE SHATTERED EMPIRE

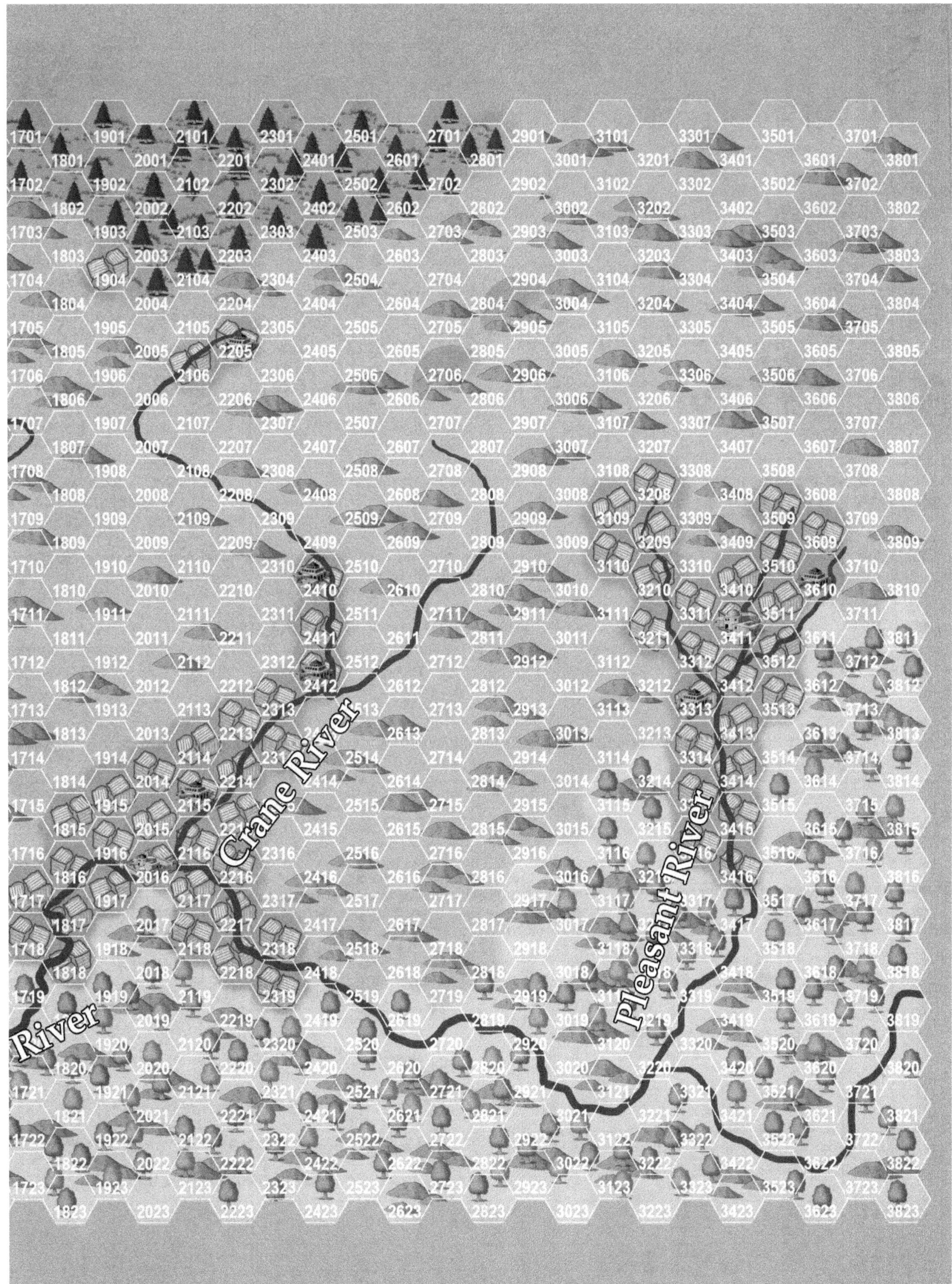

Crane River
Pleasant River
River

A libertine, she found herself otherwise engaged and unable to issue orders. The remains of her army remain inside Yal-Kirith. It consists of 3 squadrons of horse and 4 companies of foot.

The Northmen

The lands of the Empire are dominated almost entirely by the Northmen, a hearty breed of men with ebony or chocolate skin and wavy hair of brown or black, often worn long. Northmen are usually stout and often plump. While most Northmen wear tunics and leggings of wool, the nobility replace the tunic with a long robe of rich grogram with jeweled leather thongs wrapped around their forearms and torques of precious metal around their necks. Northmen favor axes and curved knives and usually wear chainmail or platemail in battle. The Northmen believe in monarchy and a great universal hierarchy with their emperor at the top, the nobility below and the commoners arrayed at the bottom. For most Northmen, this works and it is comfortable and coloring outside the lines is neither welcomed nor approved.

Encounter Key

0208.

The walled market town of Xom-Cahar is home to 5,000 men and women, mostly involved in the mining of silver and quarrying of granite from the surrounding hills, and the production of pike-armed mercenaries valued throughout the Empire. The town is situated in a deep valley of drooping pines, abandoned flooded quarries and cave bears with golden-brown fur. The town is dominated by the ebon towers of the castle of Gwisaba, enchantress and Duchess of Xom-Cahar. Gwisaba is a delicate woman with light brown skin and luxurious hair worn to her ankles and thickly braided. Gwisaba has a vast library of scrolls and dusty, leather-bound tomes that, it is said, contain all the knowledge in the world and beyond. One of these tomes, locked and bound in iron, contains a dimensional pocket in which Gwisaba keeps her treasure of 5,660 gp and 1,500 sp.

Gwisaba, Magic-User Lvl 9: HP 27; AC 9 [10]; Save 7 (5 vs. spells); CL/XP 10/1400; Special: Spells (5th). Robes, dagger, silver earrings worth 200 gp, spellbook.

0214.

Seven white apes are feasting on corpses in a rocky clearing. One of the corpses, an elderly man, is carrying a bar of silver. The silver bar is actually hollow (a dwarf or very observant human might notice that it is too light) and contains a small piece of paper on which is scrawled "Seek ye the golden pillar across the river".

White Ape: HD 4; AC 6 [13]; Atk 2 claws (1d4); Move 15; Save 13; CL/XP 4/120; Special: None.

0222.

Passing through this hex, you may come across a small cabin in the woods. The cabin consists of a single room, dingy and cluttered, with walls decorated with the most appalling bits of taxidermy you have ever seen. The cabin is home to Telyn, a broad-shouldered old woman with skin the color of mahogany, silver hair worn in a beaded net and a care-worn face. Telyn is both a cat lady (she owns at least fifteen animals of every variety one could imagine) and a genuine prophetess, touched by the goddess of the underworld, Waith. Her small painted terracotta idol of Waith appears as giant hawk with the head of a matron, hair oiled and curled into ringlets, eyes chalk white, a silver chain set with a ruby worn around her forehead. The goddess' presence can be felt in the cabin by clerics and elves as an oppressive melancholy. It was Waith that Telyn prayed to when as a maiden her heart was broken by the rascal Iulfun [0620]. Waith took pity on the girl and took away her heart, turning her into a crone and removing her ability to ever love or feel the pain of a lost love again. In the black hollow of her breast, Telyn now holds a divine spark that Waith plucked from her own breast, and it is this spark that gives her the ability to deliver prophecies. To pay for one of her prophecies, one must deliver to Telyn a cat of a breed she does not yet own.

How does Telyn's prophecy work? A player may suggest what they would like to have happen to their character, while the Referee suggests a specific problem that may befall them in the process of fulfilling that wish. Anytime either possibility comes into play, a +2 bonus it added to a dice roll (or penalty subtracted from a dice roll) that could make it come true. The "prophecy" must be specific and must be relatively near term. Thus, a player may suggest that their character will slay Princess Petal, while the Referee suggests that they may be killed by poison in the process. The player then receives a +2 bonus on attacks against Princess Petal and a -2 penalty to saves vs. poison while trying to accomplish their goal.

Rumors

When adventurers are seeking information or rumors in a settlement or from the lord of a castle, you can roll a random rumor from the table below. Each rumor is either True ("T") or False ("F") and the hex number associated with the rumor is given in brackets.

Roll	True Rumors	Roll	False Rumors
1	The emperor was undone by murder most foul!	11	A caravan of men from the Sea Lordies to the east are bringing Prince Beorwin back to claim the throne. [Hex 3819]
2	Princess Petal is not to be trusted.	12	The Temple of Four Goddesses, if you can find it, holds treasures beyond your wildest imagination. [Hex 3503]
3	The Seven Sleepers await the crack of Hell! [Hex 1510]	13	Striking steel and flint wards away bulettes. [Hex 3104]
4	There is a wishing well somewhere in the wilderness. [Hex 0303]	14	There is a chamber of horrors beneath the temple of Almerla in Valley of Tulips. [Hex 2410]
5	The Thunder god's lover dwells near the White River. [Hex 0822]	15	The imperial regalia are held in the vaults of the temple of Telos, the lord of war. [Hex 1811]
6	Farin of Xom-Iforn is the Empire's greatest swordsmith. [Hex 1607]	16	The dwellers 'neath the hills are ever the friends of men. [Hex 1103]
7	Beware the impaled god and touch not the instrument of his destruction. [Hex 2202]	17	It was a one-eyed man that killed the Emperor. [Hex 0512]
8	Candle may be the only man alive that can save the Empire from complete ruin. [Hex 2802]	18	Princess Pearl is the only princess you can trust.
9	Vheeley and Vorsey are in need of heroes! [Hex 3416]	19	Princess Peahen is the rightful empress.
10	The elven eagle riders would see the Empire fall.[Hex 3520]	20	The emperor had a secret heir in his palace.

0303.

Amidst the shattered remains of a castle is a large courtyard paved with golden-orange quartz. In the middle of the courtyard is a narrow well built of the same stone and decorated with friezes of stars, moons and the sun. A copper bucket attached to a long chain allows one to draw water from the well. By throwing a single copper piece into the well, one gains the ability to cast a *wish* within the next 24 hours. To cast a wish, they must preface it with the words "By the Sun, Moon and stars, I wish …". Each hour that passes until the person makes the wish imposes a cumulative -1 penalty to all rolls that character makes using a d20 – i.e. saving throws, attack rolls, etc. Once the wish is cast or the 24 hours is up, the accumulated penalty vanishes.

0405.

A narrow pass in the highlands has been trapped by a clan of 10 atomies. The atomies hide in small caves in the sides of the pass, the cave mouths hidden behind bits of loose foliage. The traps are spiked planks bent back so that when one trips a wire they spring out, inflicting 1d6 points of damage and causing one to go lame (half movement) for 1d4 days unless they pass a saving throw.

Atomie: HD 1d3; AC 4 [15]; Atk 1 weapon (1d3); Move 15 (F24); Save 18; CL/XP 2/30; Special: Spells (blink, entangle, invisibility (self), pass without trace, speak with animals), magic resistance (20%), surprise on 1-2 on 1d6.

0418.

A band of desperate brigands sought to use an old stone tower here as their base of operations for raiding the countryside, but instead have found themselves trapped in a place of horror. The tower stands atop a deep shaft, a well that contains an evil presence. The presence warps one's sense of reality and the surviving bandits are now mad men who think themselves princes in a palace of delights. The interior of the place is filthy and the men are slowly starving as they sup on imaginary banquets and quench their thirst with imaginary wine.

A – The inner courtyard of the tower is paved with reddish bricks and contains a well that exudes a strange, sickly sweet smell. The aforementioned well is 100 feet deep and grants access to a series of roughly cut chambers shored up with timbers. A thin layer of water on the floor in these chambers has slowly rotted the timbers, making walking through the cramped tunnels (5 feet high, 4 feet wide) dangerous. For each round of fighting in the tunnels, there is a 1 in 12 chance of a cave-in (save or be buried and suffer 3d6 damage plus 1d6 damage per round) until freed). Apparently, when the well went dry, the owners of the keep decided to dig deeper and found something they were unprepared to handle. For the tunnels and chambers beneath the tower keep show signs of ancient, crumbling ophidian masonry, distinctly the work of the serpent men (dwarves and magic-users have a 3 in 6 chance of knowing this).

A1 – As one enters this room, the water on the floor begins to rise slowly and bubble and froth. Vapors in the shape of humanoids appear on the surface and swirl around the intruders. This show – for it is a mere show – is due to a minor haunting by the spirit of a magic-user that died here many years ago. The spirit cannot harm anyone. It can be turned as though it were a 4 HD undead.

A2 – The floor of this chamber is sunken four feet below the entrance and the ceiling rises 15 feet above the floor. Three colossal cobras have been carved from stone and now hang precariously over the earthen floor. Any disturbance in the room carries the possibility (as above) of a cave-in, but will also topple the statues, causing an additional 3d6 points of damage. A wing of darkmantles lives on the ceiling above.

Darkmantles: HD 1+2; AC 4 [15]; Atk 1 grab (1d4); Move 3 (Fly 3); Save 17; CL/XP 2/30; Special: Suffocation, darkness.

A3 – A slight cave-in has left three people buried under about 3 feet of earth. Two of the bodies wear ring mail shirts (the leather straps have rotted away) and carry short swords and hammers. The third appears to

have been an academic or magic-user of some sort, judging by his robes. He carries a silver flask filled with holy water and three silver spikes, as well as a hammer. A swarm of flesh-eating beetles has infested the soil.

Flesh-Eating Beetle Swarm: HD 2; AC 7 [12]; Atk 1 swarm (1d4); Move 3; Save 16; CL/XP 3/60; Special: Covers a 20-ft diameter area, attacking all creatures in that area once per round and ignoring armor, immune to all mental effects.

A4 – This room has an undulating floor and ceiling. The southern wall appears to have caved in, for it now consists of packed earth at a 45-degree angle. Embedded in this earth is what appears to be the skeleton of a large mermaid, with extremely long and pointed finger bones and a curious crest atop its head. These demonic remains are the source of the madness in the tower above, and any in its presence must pass a saving throw each round or be struck by *confusion* for that round. Once a person has failed three such saving throws, they are struck permanently insane. The only way to destroy the corpse is to drive a silver stake into the skull and anoint the bones with holy water. Hidden within the skull is the famed *Orb of Yal-Kirith*. Any attempt to seize the Orb results in the summoning of a guardian daemon in the form of a giant bat-thing surrounded by a greenish aura of greasy smoke.

Guardian Daemon: HD 8; AC -1 [20]; Atk 1 bite (2d6) and 2 claws (1d6); Move 12; Save 8; CL/XP 11/1700; Special: Breath weapon (cone of fire 30' L x15' W, 5d6 damage), +1 or better weapon to hit, immune to acid and poison, telepathy 100', cannot move more than 20 feet away from the Orb.

B – These stables are now empty, save for the bloated corpse of a man wearing chainmail. The man's skull has been crushed by a heavy weight and rats have been nibbling on him. Two giant rats hide in the mouldering hay.

Giant Rats: HD 1d4; AC 7 [12]; Atk 1 bite (1d3); Move 12; Save 18; CL/XP A/5; Special: 5% chance of disease.

C - This antechamber is empty save for three clay jugs, each stopped with a cork. Two of the jugs contain the same mold as now dwells in the solarium [I]. The third is an *eversmoking bottle*. The stairs here lead up to level 2. The door has been jammed from the inside with two iron spikes.

D – This guardroom is inhabited by three madmen in chainmail and tattered tunics. They are staring intently at a chalk statue of a tall, thin, graceful woman with gills on her neck and a wide, rectangular hat balanced on her head. Any speaking by the adventurers is greeted with a chorus of hushes and them saying, in unison, "Quiet, brother, she is about to speak!" In fact, she is not.

Madman: HD 3+3; AC 6 [13]; Atk 1 frenzy (1d6+1); Move 15; Save 14; CL/XP 4/120; Special: Immune to mental effects.

E – This kitchen is home to a cleaver wielding man naked save for a basket worn in the manner of a crown. He is tormented by a number of giant rats that he addresses as though they are rebellious servants. At the sight of newcomers, he will command they subdue the pests and then attend to his dressing. Soiled and bloodied robes are scattered about the kitchen, along with rolls as hard as rocks and vegetables and meat in various states of decay. A side of rotten beef hangs in one corner, lousy with rot grubs. The stairs here have been trapped with a tripwire that sends a suit of platemail filled with stones crashing down the stairs (save or suffer 1d8 damage).

Madman: HD 3+3; AC 6 [13]; Atk 1 frenzy (1d6+1); Move 15; Save 14; CL/XP 4/120; Special: Immune to mental effects.

Giant Rats: HD 1d4; AC 7 [12]; Atk 1 bite (1d3); Move 12; Save 18; CL/XP A/5; Special: 5% chance of disease.

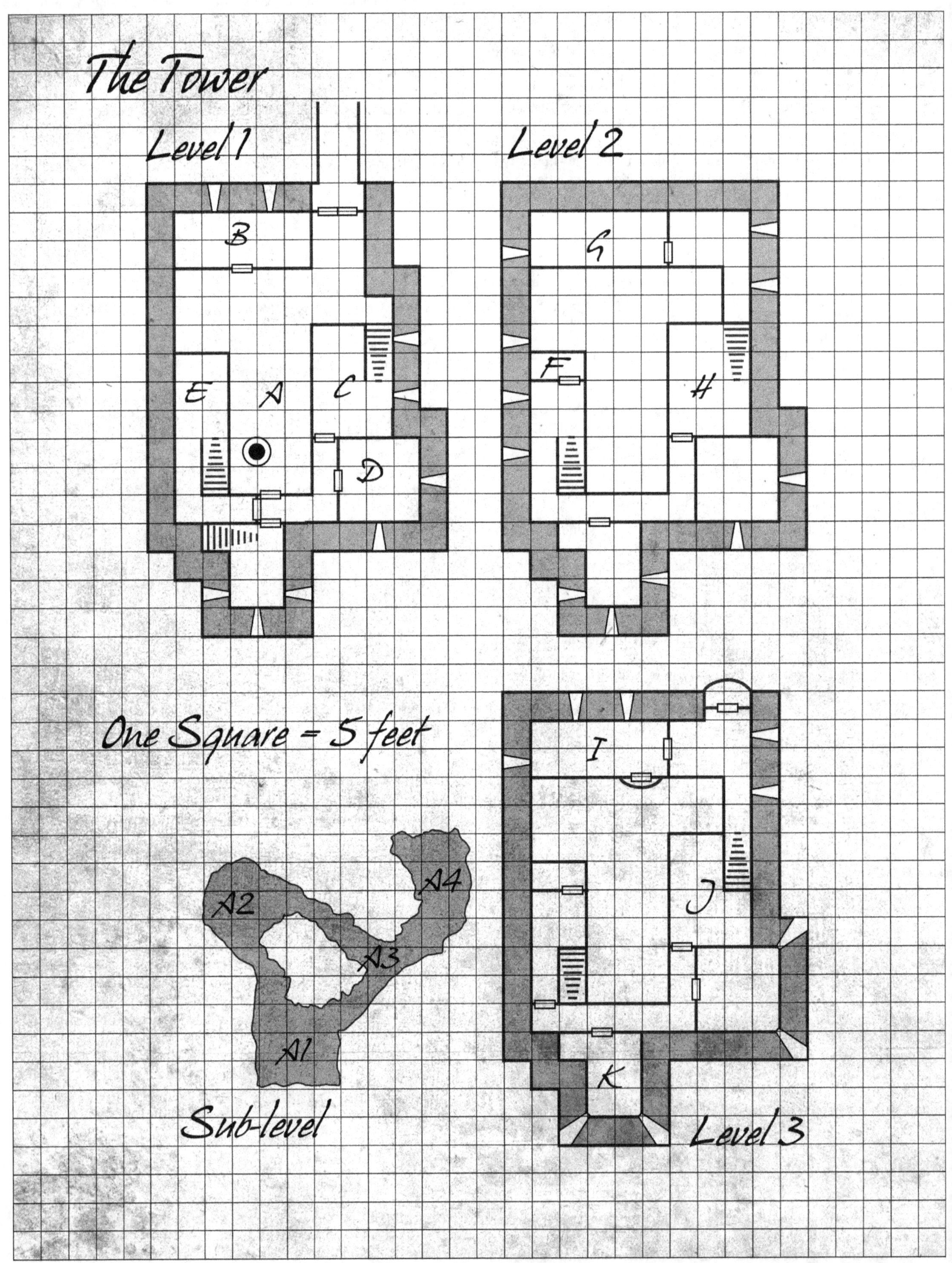

The Tower
Level 1
Level 2
B
E A C
D
One Square = 5 feet
A2
A4
A3
A1
Sub-level
I
J
K
Level 3
G
F H

Rot Grubs: One must save to avoid contacting these vermin. If this check is failed, the grubs penetrate the skin. Once this occurs, the victim may make a saving throw. If successful, he notices strange burrowing below the surface of his skin. Each round thereafter, a saving throw must be made. If failed, the victim sustains 2d6 points of damage. At 0 hit points, the victim dies. The grubs then look for a new host. During the first two rounds, the grubs can be killed by applying flame to or by cutting open the affected skin. The flame or cutting does 2d6 points of damage to the victim. After the second round, only a cure disease spell can save the victim.

F – This water closet is terribly foul smelling, due to it having been stopped up with the corpse of a bandit. The effluence within has spawned several immature otyughs that look like slugs with several small tentacles. The creatures aren't dangerous and in fact the sheath of slime around their bodies can be used to cure any disease (treat as one *potion of cure disease*).

G – This room was used as an officer's mess. The table now serves to hold the corpse of a former sub-chief of the bandits, who is secured to it with heavy ropes. The mutilation of his body and the sated looks on the bloody faces of the five bandits in the room tell a grisly tale.

Madman (5): HD 3+3; AC 6 [13]; Atk 1 frenzy (1d6+1); Move 15; Save 14; CL/XP 4/120; Special: Immune to mental effects.

H – This large hall was used as the mess for the common soldiery of the tower. The tables and chairs have been splintered. Ten crazed bandits now appear to be sleeping here under soiled blankets, but in truth have had a good portion of their strength drained by a pack of four shadow rats that inhabits the room. A leather sack beneath the rubble holds 400 gp and a silver dagger in a sheath decorated with gold embroidery (worth 80 gp).

Weakened Madman: HD 1+1; AC 6 [13]; Atk 1 frenzy (1d4); Move 9; Save 17; CL/XP 2/30; Special: Immune to mental effects.

Shadow Rat: HD 1; AC 3 [16]; Atk 1 bite (1d4 plus 1d3 strength); Move 15 (C9); Save 17; CL/XP 4/120; Special: Disease, strength damage, incorporeal, shadow blend, surprise on 1-3 on 1d6.

I - The solarium is inhabited by a reddish-black mold with a psychic hive mind that allows it to read thoughts, induce hallucinations and lure people to come sit on the floor, backs against the wall, that they might be consumed by the mold. Three bloated corpses are in such a position already and in an advanced state of decay. The mad men describe these corpses as the "sleeping maidens" they are sworn to protect. One of the corpses holds a bone map case that is empty save for a small cat's-eye marble that, if placed on the floor, rolls directly towards the most valuable treasure within 100 feet.

The mold's mind-dominating power can be defeated with a successful saving throw; anyone failing the saving throw will try to join the "princesses" beside the wall, and will fight anyone keeping them from doing so. The mold itself can only be killed with fire, taking no appreciable damage from weapons or non-fire spells.

0512.

A band of 250 starving refugees from farms surrounding Yal-Zanath is scavenging in these hills. They are under the protection of three clerics, Father Udach One-Eye, Sister Cwall and Brother Bjarn. The clerics are desperate to keep the people fed, which is difficult since the farmers are unskilled at living in the wilderness. There is a 1 in 6 chance that adventurers become entangled in one of the refugees' crude snares (1d4 damage) while moving through this hex. One of the refugees is a sage named Malarine who served in the citadel of Princess Peahen.

Father Udach, Cleric Lvl 5: HP 20; AC 2 [17]; Save 11 (9 vs. paralysis and poison); CL/XP 5/240; Special: Banish undead, spells (2/2). Platemail, shield, helm decorated with peacock feathers (worth 10 gp), mace, holy symbol of Vephus in the form of a gold mask worn over the face.

Sister Cwall, Cleric Lvl 3: HP 10; AC 2 [17]; Save 13 (11 vs. paralysis and poison); CL/XP 3/60; Special: Banish undead, spells (2). Platemail, shield, mace, throwing hammer, holy symbol of Vephus, indigo cape.

Brother Bjarn, Cleric Lvl 2: HP 6; AC 4 [15]; Save 14 (12 vs. paralysis and poison); CL/XP 2/30; Special: Banish undead, spells (1). Chainmail, shield, warhammer, sling, holy symbol of Vephus.

0523.

A deep, dank pit (30 feet deep) has been bored into the ground here. The pit is covered by loose branches and a tendriculos lies at its bottom. Lodged within the tendriculos is a brass bust of the Emperor Brodred (worth 6,000 gp).

Tendriculos: HD 8; AC 4[15]; Atk 2 tendrils (1d6), 1 bite (2d6); Move 9; Save 8; CL/XP 9/1100; Special: Swallow whole.

0614.

An onion-shaped hot air balloon has been anchored via a chain to a wooden post driven into the top of a hill. The balloon is one of a fleet of six now commanded by Princess Petal. Deployed a week ago, the poor observers have been stuck in the balloon ever since a gang of twenty zombies became attracted to the object and congregated on the hill. The balloon is colored bright blue, with a gilded gondola in the shape of a falcon hanging beneath it. It holds six men, four men-at-arms and two cartographers equipped with spy glasses and maps of the surrounding area. As battles have moved armies hither and yon, this balloon has been forgotten and no help is on its way. The balloon is not really intended for navigation of the air currents. Such movements are always quite random (without the aid of magic) and carry a 1 in 6 chance of the balloon coming apart each day.

Zombie: HD 2; AC 8 [11] or with shield 7[12]; Atk 1 weapon or strike (1d8); Move 6; Save 16; CL/XP 2/30; Special: Immune to sleep and charm.

0620.

As one pokes their way through a thick wood, they come upon a most extraordinary fortress; a sprawling castle of opaque green glass with flying buttresses and domed towers. From the top of the highest tower to the lower walls, there are fountains of sparkling water pouring like waterfalls and forming a large lake. The lake is ringed by sycamores and hawthorns and coursed by dozens of gentle white boats, long and graceful, from which brown-skinned dwarves fling nets and pull in large, golden fish. The dwarves once ventured out from the green castle to work platinum mines in the surrounding woods, mines hidden beneath large oaks and guarded by brown bears. Now, they and their master, the archmage Iulfun, while away the time feasting on fish and exotic fruits and vegetables grown in the glass towers and drinking the sparkling ethereal waters that condense on the domes each night as the castle's spires scrape against the Ethereal Plane. Iulfun and his followers, twenty dwarves and their wives and children, are convinced that the war now ravaging the Empire is a sign of the foretold end of the world. Iulfun has many wonders lurking in his castle (not to mention a few dangers) as well as a vault of magic mirrors in which he hides a treasure of 1,690 gp and seven miniature oxen with jeweled horns. The oxen are worth 150 gp each).

Iulfun, Magic-User Lvl 11: HP 45; AC 9 [10]; Save 5 (3 vs. spells); CL/XP 11/1700; Special: Spells (4/4/4/3/3). Staff, silver dagger, three darts tucked up his sleeve, luxurious robes, white headband emblazoned with eldritch glyphs in gold thread (worth 100 gp), spellbook.

0707.

A tent city of 500 war refugees has been set up on a broad meadow with a bubbling brook now fouled by human waste. The local wildlife are slowly being driven away and the people are becoming desperate for

11

food. Adventurers are likely to be mobbed by men and women looking for food and weapons. Among the refugees is a curly-haired gentleman with a broad smile and pleasant mien. Lorbes by name, he was a merchant of Yal-Zanath [1007] who fled with only the shirt on his back. He has become the de facto leader of the mob and is now doing his best to divert their attention from their hopeless situation by turning the people against one another. Three bodies, partially charred, hang from a tall sycamore tree in the meadow's center (the tree is also slightly charred) – Lorbes accused them of hording acorns. Lorbes now has the refugees building a shrine to Vilmarra, the goddess of vengeance, in a bid to petition her for divine assistance. He has set himself up as the high priest and is on the hunt looking for a suitable sacrifice.

0711.

A road house here as escaped destruction in the raging war – at least so far. The house is constructed of stone, with walls 3 feet thick and a tiled roof. An 8-ft tall wall surrounds a courtyard inhabited by a dozen swine. There is a well of sweet water in the courtyard and a stone stable containing seven horses. The road house is owned by Murvyn, a despicable old warrior who now hosts about twenty wealthy refugees (each has 1d6 x 25 gp left in their purse) doing their best to pass the war in the relative safety of this roadhouse. Murvyn employs three serving wenches, a halfling cook who dreams of traveling south and a bitter old dwarf who works in the stables. An iron grate in the floor of the great hearth hides a trapdoor to a secret cellar. The cellar abuts the roadhouse's wine cellar and contains three rooms dug from the earth and clad in red brick. These rooms now house the Princess Peahen and three of her swordsmen. All four are resting here before continuing south. The halfling cook has discovered their presence, but has kept his silence with promises that they will take him along, provided he raids the pantry first. The princess plans to leave two days after the adventurer's arrive (as luck would have it).

Princess Peahen, Fighting-Woman Lvl 7: HP 22; AC 4 [15]; Save 8; CL/XP 7/600, Special: Multiple attacks, parry. Chainmail, buckler, longsword, silver dagger, fox-lined cloak held with a hematite pin (worth 125 gp) .

Swordsmen, Fighting-Men Lvl 4: HP 4d8; AC 4 [15]; Save 11; CL/XP 4/120, Special: Multiple attacks, parry. Chainmail, shield, longsword, dagger, light crossbow.

Murvyn, Fighting-Man Lvl 3: HP 18; AC 9 [10]; Save 12; CL/XP 3/60, Special: Multiple attacks, parry. Club, dagger.

0716.

There is a town here that fell to a siege by the forces of Princess Petal many weeks ago. The town's walls have been breached next to the gatehouse, which was burned badly, though most of the town remains intact. While most of the town's population was carried into slavery by Petal's army, the soldiery was summarily executed, their bodies tossed into the wide moat that surrounds the town and buried with a thin layer of dirt and gravel. In many places the rotting bodies are exposed, or have been exposed by the action of ghouls and other carrion creatures. Thousands of ravens line the walls and rats are thick around the moat. A pack of ghouls has burrowed in from below and is so sated with carrion that, sitting atop the walls singing at night, they will almost certainly ignore intruders. The town was once known for its factories that rendered beets down into sugary syrup. The town's citadel shows signs of terrible damage and burning and what remains of the furniture has been turned over and splintered in what appears to be an act of looting. In fact, the soldiers were searching for clues to the whereabouts of the imperial regalia so desired by Princess Petal. A band of seven soldiers and the citadel's bailiff have found their way into a hiding place behind a secret door in the donjon. They are running low on food, but fear the ghouls too much to leave their hiding place yet.

0718.

As the adventurers enter a clearing, they discover a pack of 8 wolves.

Three of them are feasting on a human body, while the others look intently into the branches of a tree where three small children are hiding, apparently placed there by their deceased father. The children are Ossior (male, age 12, 3 hp), Angwen (female, age 9, 2 hp) and Brellyr (female, age 6, 1 hp). Ossior carries a hand axe and a dagger. His father has a full waterskin and a backpack containing sleeping rolls, a week of iron rations and a letter written in a flowing script from the wizard Iulfun [0620] imploring his brother Gwirig to come stay in his tower until the end of the world.

Wolves: HD 2+2; AC 7 [12]; Atk 1 bite (1d4+1); Move 18; Save 16; CL/XP 2/30; Special: None.

0803.

Xom-Yeric is a small town of 2,500 people. It is carved from the granite of the hills that flank the Shining River. Xom-Yeric is known for its highly trained city guard, mineral baths surrounded by lush gardens of magnolias, anemones and tethered monkeys with pink faces and long fur the color of toasted acorns, dwarven jewelers from the mystic south and an ancient castle of gray stone set on a rocky island in the midst of the river. The island is connected to the rest of the town via a stone causeway composed of three earth elementals bound by ancient magic. Xom-Yeric is governed by Caranth, a minor sorcerer and servant of Princess Pearl. Caranth is a pitiable toady, wracked by self-doubt and given to wild bursts of energy and "genius" that ultimately come to nothing. He has very dark, brown eyes, wispy black hair rapidly turning gray and a deceptively athletic build (he favors long swims in the morning and bouts of fencing that his instructors usually let him win). Almerla, the goddess of healing, is the patron deity of Xom-Yeric and has a large temple and hospice in the town. The town's treasure consists of 1,680 sp, 2,580 gp and a malachite dagger worth 400 gp hidden inside an enchanted terracotta lion that belches forth the treasure when one tickles its chin with a feather.

Caranth, Magic-User Lvl 5: HP 14; AC 9 [10]; Save 11 (9 vs. spells); CL/XP 4/120; Special: Spells (4/2/1). Staff bedecked with eagle feathers and a nugget of silver (worth 20 gp), silver dagger, spellbook.

0809.

The hills here are haunted by four highwaymen. The highwaymen are garbed in black ring armor and they cover their faces with black kerchiefs that obscure the top of their faces. They carry light crossbows and long swords and are mounted on black chargers. The leader of the highwaymen is Intinus, a belligerent man with a golden voice and angelic face who was once a herald in the employ of Princess Peahen. The highwaymen have a lair 2 miles to the east in a forest cave. They've protected the cave with a lasso trap (save or be suspended from a 20-ft tall tree and suffer 1d10 points of damage from the jostling). They have amassed a treasure of 960 sp, 290 gp and two enameled terracotta cups (worth 160 gp each) hidden beneath a loose rock in the cave. The cups were taken from Peahen's palace. One of them still has dried traces of poison in it which remains deadly if liquid is put into the cup and then drank.

Highwayman: HD 3+1; AC 6 [13]; Atk 1 weapon (1d8); Move 12 (24 on horseback); Save 14; CL/XP 3/60; Special: Surprise on roll of 1-4 on 1d6, +1 to initiative.

0822.

The woods here are dominated by a 150 foot tall white oak with a diameter of 120 feet. Most days, a nymph can be found sitting in the high boughs of the oak, combing her satin tresses with a comb of serpentine. The nymph has nut-brown skin, golden eyes and her hair is 8 feet long. She is called Mayblossom, but discovering her identity is exceptionally difficult for she speaks little and answers most communication with no more than a haughty laugh. Mayblossom has reason to be haughty, for she has recently caught the eye of Clarn, the god of thunder and storms. In fact, there is a 1 in 20 chance that Clarn is visiting the nymph. Clarn appears as a stocky man with bronzed skin and wild, auburn hair. He wears nothing but an iron crown and a bearskin cloak. He rides through the heavens on a sinuous dragon called Isota. Isolta has brilliant white scales and a forked

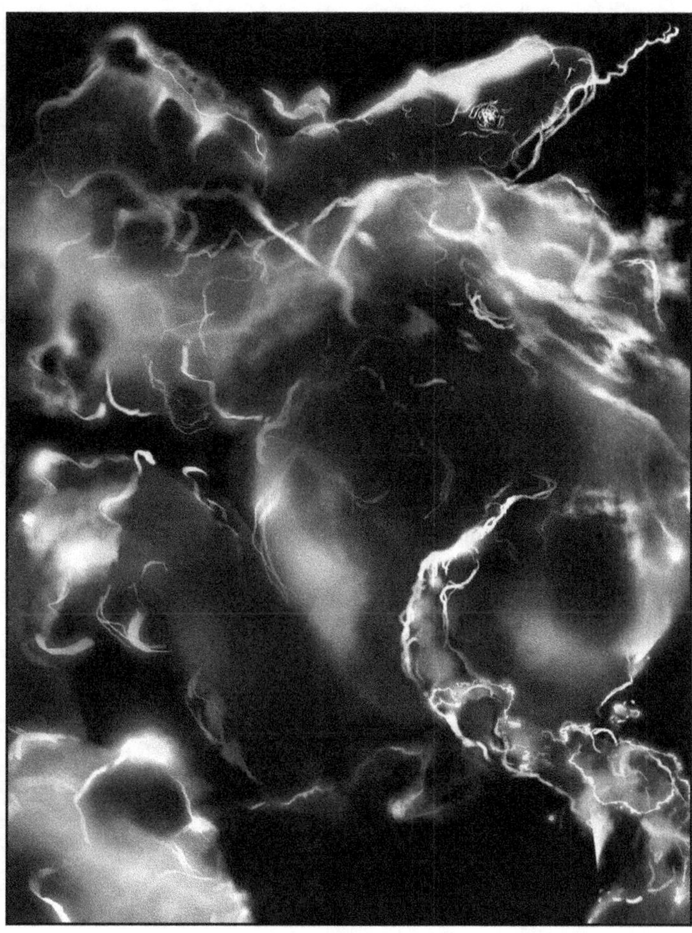

on his pyre. Those who would investigate the pyres will discover to their chagrin that the lords' spirits are still quite active and manifest as a storm of fire. The swords can be reforged into *+1 blades* that force their owners to seek battle at every opportunity (saving throw to resist the impulse), but only a forge kindled with fire taken from the aforementioned storm of fire.

Fire Elemental: HD 12; AC 2 [17]; Atk 1 strike (2d6); Move 12; Save 3; CL/XP 13/2300; Special: Ignite materials.

1001.

A weird stone promontory here resembles two titanic humanoids locked in combat, hands upon one another's shoulders as though wrestling. In fact, they are the corporeal forms of two earth spirits that were summoned and then dispatched long ago during a duel between two wizards. These stony "corpses" are now riddled with holes created by a dozen thoqqua (1d4 are encountered on a roll of 1 on 1d6 made each hour spent investigating the bodies). Located in the chest cavity of each elemental, if one can get to it, is what appears to be a ruby-red geode worth 500 gp each and useful in powerful elemental magic, including the creation of a stone golem.

Thoqqua: HD 3; AC 2 [17]; Atk 1 slam (1d6 + fire); Move 12 (B9); Save 14; CL/XP 4/120; Special: Immune to fire, touch inflicts 1d6 points of fire damage.

1007.

In the center of many miles of razed and empty land there stands the rotting corpse of the once great city of Yal-Zanath. It is surrounded by the abandoned earthworks and camps of the besieging army that destroyed it. The walls of the city, which stand 40 feet tall and are up to 20 feet thick, have been breached in two different places now clogged with corpses in various states of decay. The gatehouse towers have been burned to a smoldering ruin and much of the city has shared the same fate. All of the city's temples have been looted and desecrated, their priests crushed beneath their own toppled idols.

Yal-Zanath was the seat of Princess Peahen's power. Her castle has been left practically untouched, but the invading army did not leave a garrison. Almost all of the city-state's populace and wealth was carried away – any ranger can read the tracks left behind by thousands of civilians and hundreds of oxcarts loaded with plunder. All that remains to walk the city's streets, covered as they are with ash and rubble, are stray dogs eating the unburied dead, desperate orphans (treat as thieves of 1st to 4th level) and packs of hunting ghouls (1 in 6 chance of an encounter each hour with 1d4+1 ghouls).

The citadel still holds Yal-Zanath's grand vizier, a haggard looking man called Admund, and a garrison of thirty archers. While the mad Admund lords it over "his domain" in the name of the missing Princess Peahen, his men spend the day raiding the citadels' vast wine cellars. They fear the ghouls and never leave the walls of the citadel. The dungeons beneath the citadel still hold dozens of starving prisoners.

1010.

Xom-Devyn is a modest town surrounded by fields of golden grain swaying in the wind. The town is known for its potters, who glaze their lovely pots and vases with a polychromatic glaze that has hypnotic qualities. Such pots are favored by those of strong wills, decorating their homes with them to capture the weak-willed and unwary. The town has towering walls of golden-brown marble, a tremendous gatehouse and a stout citadel ruled by Nipharna, a thin, dimwitted countess with dazzling green eyes. Niphana is an animal lover and has banned hunting within her domain. Only butchers that hold a special charter from the Countess are permitted to kill animals for their meat, making meat especially expensive in Xom-Devyn. Nipharna is vain in the extreme, always appearing in rich robes and bedecked with jewels. Her handmaids are the most beautiful women of her city and her servants are all enslaved halflings from the far west, renowned for their golden hair and skin. She dresses them in velvet robes and jeweled collars, sandals and gloves, and she treats them as much like living works of art as servants.

Thieves throughout the Empire tell stories, only half-believed, of the

---

blue tongue. When Clarn is not in residence, he leaves behind three 20-ft long constrictors with white scales to protect her.

Mayblossom dwells "inside" the tree in an extra-dimensional manse. The manse consists of sixteen rooms, all clad in bronzewood panels and floors with arched ceilings and exposed rafters. The furnishings are plush and ornate. One cannot enter the manse without the help of Mayblossom, who must hold their hand as she passes into the tree, or without being a druid casting *plant doorway*. Her only treasure is a *+1 staff* carved from oak and inlaid with dozens of crystal butterflies.

Mayblossom: Nymph: HD 3 (9 hp); AC 9 [10]; Atk none; Move 12; Save 14; CL/XP 5/240; Special: Sight causes blindness or death.

Clarn, God of Thunder: HD 20 (110 hp); AC -3 [22]; Atk 2 slams (2d8+2); Move 18; Save 2; CL/XP 27/5500; Special: Immune to electricity, cold and fire, magic resistance (75%), spells as a 15th level druid, cast lightning bolt 3/day, only harmed by +2 or better weapons.

Isota, White Wyrm: HD 7 (70 hp); AC 2 [17]; Atk 2 claws (1d6) and bite (2d8); Move 9 (F24); Save 9; CL/XP 11/1700; Special: Breathes cold, magic resistance (40%), only harmed by +1 or better weapons.

Lightning Serpent: HD 5; AC 5 [14]; Atk 2 bites (1d8); Move 12 (C12); Save 12; CL/XP 7/600; Special: Quickness (2 attacks per round), those hit by a bite must pass a save or be constricted for 1d8 damage per round, can become a 3 dice lightning bolt once per day.

0912.

A wide meadow is littered with three stone pyres, apparently the last resting place of a trio of knights who died fighting the forces of Princess Petal. Each of the knights possessed a sword, now snapped in two, that lies fabulous treasure vaults beneath the citadel of Xom-Devyn. More than a few thieves have sought out these vaults, falling prey to the guardsmen of Xom-Devyn or the trained cougars that are given free run of the citadel after dark.

1103.

A cave mouth set in the ground in this hex leads to a great cavern. During the day, for a few hours, sunlight filters in through the hole, falling upon a bronze trapdoor that reflects the light. The trapdoor is set atop the tower of a ruined castle located inside the cave. The cavern is 80 feet in height and 300 feet in diameter. The subterranean gatehouse is a piece of monolithic architecture, carved into the western wall of the cavern where a tunnel leaves the cavern and descends into the underworld. The other walls of the cavern are terraced and hold hundreds of bits of pottery and a few complete terracotta vessels filled with the bones of dead Carudaa. The Carudaa once lived in this subterranean fortress, guarding the cavern, which they used as a communal burial ground, from incursions from deeper within the earth. The gatehouse is now abandoned, save for a small band of goblins dwelling beneath the trapdoor. The goblins tend growths of chunky, white fungus and hunt rats in the great cavern and avoid the remainder of the gatehouse. The goblins have reddish skins covered by a translucent slime, like that of a snail, and large eyes.

The tunnel that leads from the cavern is barred by a rusty portcullis that can no longer be raised. The archway is mirrored. The mirrors emit a soft, white light inside of which there is a strange woman held in suspended animation. The goblins fear the woman and avoid this area. The woman, Agnes, is a centaur that stands about 6 feet tall and wears chainmail barding and a chainmail shirt and carries a shield and battle axe.

Beyond the portcullis are the caverns of a band of fifteen trolls, hermits that attempt to kill one another on sight except during the one day "mating season" that occurs during the dead of winter. The trolls have pallid skin, long, clawed fingers and toes, slit yellow eyes, no noses, gaping, toothy mouths and stringy, gray-green hair. It is said that beyond the troll caves there is an abandoned subterranean city of the Carudaa.

Troll: HD 6+3; AC 4 [15]; Atk 2 claws (1d4), 1 bite (1d8); Move 12; Save 11; CL/XP 8/800; Special: Regenerate 3hp/round.

Goblin: HD 1d6hp; AC 6 [13]; Atk 1 weapon (1d6); Move 9; Save 18; CL/XP B/10; Special: -1 to hit in sunlight.

Agnes, Centaur Fighter Lvl 6: HP 30; AC 4 [15]; Save 9; CL/XP 6/400, Special: Multiple attacks, parry. Chainmail, shield, battleaxe, lance, light crossbow.

1109.

Three creepy gentlemen swathed in black robes and carrying silver hatchets are making their way across a battlefield strewn with corpses. The men carry sacks laden with their pickings and jars and vials hang from their belts filled with fluids and other bits and pieces. The men are, of course, necromancers – unsavory little nits of only minor ability that are plotting to make a patchwork man, one of them having come into possession of a partial manual while looting the tent of a soldier-magician in a burning camp. The men are called Conch, Nellon and Odoar, identifiable by the yellow canary always on the shoulder of Conch, the smell of beets that lingers about Nellon and Odoar's twisted left foot. All three are avowed cowards and possessed of an enviable gift of gab. Their silver tongues have extricated from many more scrapes than has their magic.

Conch, Magic-User Lvl 2: HP 6; AC 9 [10]; Save 14 (12 vs. spells); CL/XP 1/15; Special: Spells (2). Ebon staff, dagger, three darts, spellbook, crushed velvet robes (soiled and tattered, worth 10 gp).

Nellon, Magic-User Lvl 3: HP 5; AC 9 [10]; Save 13 (11 vs. spells); CL/XP 2/30; Special: Spells (2/1). Dagger, three darts, wide straw hat, large hoop earring (gold-plated, worth 5 gp), linen robe with sable collar (worth 10 gp).

Odoar, Magic-User Lvl 2: HP 7; AC 9 [10]; Save 14 (12 vs. spells); CL/XP 1/15; Special: Spells (2). Two daggers, three darts, spellbook, padded doublet embroidered with silver spiders, leggings, high leather boots.

1118.

Where there is strife, death and human desperation, you will find demons. One enterprising hezrou called Saetullulios has arrived in the guise of a trader to further the interests of chaos. He has taken the guise of Etheke, a rotund woman with ochre skin and shoulder-length, wavy brown hair. Etheke is accompanied by her two "sons", manes demons in disguise. The children are unusually quiet and sullen and answer to the names Affyn and Robar. She and the boys travel in a gypsy wagon pulled by a slobbering ox (a polymorphed gorgon). The wagon is painted in bright colors. The sides contain shelves holding bottles of every color and shape imaginable behind locked iron gates.

The wagon has a rear door (*wizard locked*) that leads into what appears to be an endless corridor of amethyst light. As one walks down the corridor, they lose a point of constitution with each step. At 0 constitution, they die and their soul is sucked into the walls of the amethyst corridor, and thus into the possession of the hezrou. Lost constitution returns if one departs the corridor at the rate of 1 point per hour.

The bottles contain potions that Saetullulios sells for ridiculously low prices. The potions work as advertised, but they contain damned spirits that attempt, over the course of several days, to possess the imbiber. Each day, the person must pass a saving throw or gain 1d6 "possession points". When these possession points are greater than the person's wisdom score, they have been possessed by a chaotic spirit.

Hezrou: HD 28; AC 0 [19]; Atk 2 claws (1d3), 1 bite (2d8); Move 9 (Fly 14); Save 6; CL/XP 11/1700; Special: Magic resistance 50%, demonic magical powers.

Manes: HD 1; AC 5 [14]; Atk 2 claws (1d2), 1 bite (1d4); Move 5; Save 18; CL/XP 2/30; Special: Half damage from non-magic weapons.

1211.

There is a steep gully clogged with creeping vegetation in this hex. Large copper pipes poke out of the sides of the gully, disgorging water into the gully and providing a home for killer frogs. A single stone bridge, heavily weathered, spans the gully. A small stone cottage is constructed in the middle of the bridge. The stone cottage is the home of Fridebria (3 hp), a pleasant wise woman known for her pet wolf, Grius (6 hp), her excellent dumplings and her skill with potions. The potions are baked into the dumplings – one eats the potions instead of drinking them – and she is quite willing to trade a potion for a service or interesting bauble (but never something as vulgar as money). She adores killer frog legs, so a frog hunt it usually a sure avenue to getting a potion.

1223.

Far to the south of the White River, in a mountainous land of many rivers, a tribe of aquatic elves has forged a great kingdom. The kingdom consists of several large lakes created when an ancient people (perhaps the ophidians) dammed many rivers. The elves, who call themselves the Tevala, have expanded this kingdom with more and larger dams. They collect tribute from the folk who dwell on the shores of their lakes, and while they are haughty and arrogant, they are competent rulers.

Hearing of the trouble to the north, one ambitious prince by the name of Jlun has assembled an army of elves and tributary men who establish a foothold in the forested hill country. This army consists of ten squadrons of aquatic elves (five squadrons of heavy infantry, three squadrons of crossbowmen and two crews guiding giant snails with black and gold striped shells bearing lightning projectors). In addition, there are four squadrons of human skirmishers and two squadrons of human scouts led by the ranger Aglan. The lake men (as they are called) have ochre skin and curly black hair.

The aquatic elves wear coats of silvery scales (treat as chainmail), onion-domed helms of ground and polished river glass (filled with water and connected via copper tubing to brass water tanks on their backs). The heavy infantry are armed with tridents while the crossbowmen carry light crossbows and short swords. The human skirmishers carry javelins, short swords and shields and the scouts wear leather armor and carry longbows and short swords.

Should the aquatic army reach the White River it will lay siege to Yal-Garok and possibly change the course of the war of succession.

Jlun, Aquatic Elf Fighter/Magic-User Lvl 6/6: HP 25; AC 9 [10]; Save 9 (8 vs. spells); CL/XP 5/240; Special: Spells (4/2/2), darkvision 60 ft., find secret door on 4 in 6, immune to paralysis from ghouls, multiple attacks, parry. Trident, serrated dagger, light crossbow, spellbook.

Aglan, Ranger Lvl 5: HP 30; AC 4 [15]; Save 10; CL/XP 6/400; Special: Tracking, alertness, +5 damage vs giants and goblin-types. Scale armor, shield, light crossbow, longsword, throwing axe.

1305.

Herennyn, a vanquished general and his war weary soldiers have sought shelter here in a grove of oaks. The general once served the Princess Peahen. His army made a brave assault on the forces of Petal as they besieged the city of Yal-Zarnath, but they were betrayed and found themselves trapped in a pincer movement. Only the general and his personal guard, a squadron of knights and their servants, escaped. They have set up a camp here, erecting what pavilions they had and putting their servants to the task of digging a defensive ditch and erecting a small fence. The seventeen servants are all trained as men-at-arms, six of them being archers. The soldiers are running short on supplies and their servants are seriously considering falling on their masters one night and stealing away into the highlands.

Herennyn, Fighting-Man Lvl 7: HP 30; AC 2 [17]; Save 8; CL/XP 7/600, Special: Multiple attacks, parry. Platemail, shield, battleaxe, dagger, bloody bandages around head, ivory trinkets entwined in beard (worth 20 gp).

1315.

A chasm cuts through the hills here, forming a crude highway between Yal-Garok [2016] and the ruined town in [0716]. Some sections of the highway are paved, but much of it is washed out, pitted and a completely misery to travel. More importantly, the highway is haunted. A cave tomb near the middle of the chasm's length holds the body of Saint Sirth of the Wagging Finger, an infamous moralist who saw chaos and entropy everywhere he looked. In his fitful rest, he has become a covey of shadows that play against the walls of the chasm in the daytime. As people walk through the chasm, the shadows reach into their minds and put on shadow plays that reveal their innermost thoughts, especially what they truly think of their companions – sometimes exaggerated a bit for effect. Merchants that use the chasm have become used to these shadow plays and make sure to hock a nice wad of spit on the bronze plaque that marks the tomb of Saint Sirth.

1417.

A small, stone shrine is situated here atop a wooded hill. The shrine is made of white limestone and was once faced with white marble that has mostly crumbled away. The exterior of the shrine is choked with five assassin vines. There are shallow puddles of oily water on the floor of the shrine, helping to obscure a secret compartment in the floor containing a gold icon of Almerla, the healing goddess. The icon is worth 100 gp.

Assassin Vine: HD 7; AC 5 [14]; Atk 1 vine (1d6+1); Move 1; Save 9; CL/XP 8/800; Special: animate plants.

1502.

An army has camped here under the command of Wesdas, a wild eyed, pale-skinned druidess from the mountainous country to the north. Identifiable by her height (she is quite tall) and her horned helm (the horns are made of leather, the helm of bronze), she was forced to tangle with a number of wandering undead in her wooded valley and decided to strike south to discover the source of the abominations. She is accompanied by the ranger lord Dumnert and his stalwart followers, two companies of longbowmen. The men are terribly loyal to their lord, but they fear the undead and would prefer to return to their homes in the north and hole up in their houses rather than drag their women and children into the heart of the fighting.

Wesdas, Druid Lvl 8: HP 40; AC 6 [13]; Save 8 (6 vs. fire); CL/XP 9/1100; Special: Spells (4/3/2/1), first mysteries, shapechange, immune to fey charms. Leather armor (in the form of bands wound around her limbs and torso over a white tunic), shield, spear, sling, mistletoe.

Dumnert, Ranger Lvl 6: HP 50; AC 6 [13]; Save 9; CL/XP 7/600; Special: Tracking, alertness, +6 damage vs giants and goblin-types. Leather armor (quilted hauberk with steel studs), shield emblazoned with green dragon, longbow, dagger, longsword, silver ring worth 60 gp.

1510.

At the top of a rugged hill ringed with trees with blood red bark there is a vertical shaft 15 feet deep that leads into a 20-ft diameter cavern. The cavern is occupied by seven men of Herculean dimensions in ornate platemail and armed with two-handed swords. The Seven Sleepers, as they are called, snooze under the guard of a massive black mastiff with a leather collar from which hangs a gold medal embossed with the face of a horned god. This medal is intelligent and can speak, directing the dog and casting spells as a 7th level magic-user. The sleepers can be awakened only by the sounding of the great bell atop the temple of Vephus the sun god in Yal-Garok. Legend says they will awaken when the Crack of Hell opens wide and vomits demons over the face of the earth.

Seven Sleepers: HD 10; AC 2 [17]; Atk 1 weapon (2d6+2); Move 9; Save 5; CL/XP 12/2000; Special: Immune to fear, dispel evil 1/day, double damage against chaotic creatures, magic resistance (10%).

Black Mastiff: HD 8 (60 hp); AC 2 [17]; Atk 1 bite (2d6); Move 12; Save 8; CL/XP 12/2000; Special: Only harmed by +1 or better weapons, magic resistance (10%), cast spells as 7th level magic-user.

1513.

A strange cavern pierces a hillside here. The cavern entrance is 25 feet tall and 13 feet wide and sealed with what appears to be wax several feet thick. The wax is yellow-white in color and, at night, glows as though bright lights are lit inside the cavern. The waxy substance comes from a hive of subterranean bees – drones of Veluu, the goddess of destruction. The drones are as large as pit bulls and look like wingless bees with stretched, humanoid faces and empty eyes that, when opened, emit a piercing shriek. The bees live deep in the cavern. Their honey is collected by the priests of Veluu, who occupy the nearer portions of the caverns. The main cavern holds their glory, the War Wheel of Veluu. The War Wheel is built in their goddess' image, and serves as both a supernatural engine of war and an idol. The wheel is made of steel and is 16 feet in diameter and 6 feet wide. The goddess' face forms each of the wheel's hubs and her arms its spokes. The wheel is a magic item that is activated by the sacrifice of seven virtuous warriors. Six such warriors have already been captured and are held in the caverns.

The priests of Veluu are twenty men and women (1st level clerics) who dress in sable coats and wear leather skullcaps. They wear armor of metal scales (treat as chainmail) under their coats. Their high priestess, Sabrank, is a ponderous woman with a deceptively friendly face. She replaces the leather skullcap of the acolytes with a steel helm and wears platemail beneath her sable robes.

Once the Wheel of Veluu is activated, it will be released from the cavern to smash everything in its path, the priests following in its path to dedicate its victims to the glory of Veluu. Animated with a dim sentience, the device is truly terrible to behold.

Sabrank, Cleric Lvl 8: HP 35; AC 2 [17]; Save 8 (6 vs. paralysis and poison); CL/XP 9/1100; Special: Banish undead, spells (2/2/2/2/2). Black platemail, spiked shield (1d4 damage), flanged mace, unholy symbol (silver skull with human blood sealed inside).

War Wheel of Veluu: HD 14 (56 hp); AC 0 [19]; Atk special; Move 15; Save 3; CL/XP 18/3800; Special: Can attack up, forward and back with cones of fire (5d6 damage, 30-ft range), can expel clouds of poison gas (save or die) to left or right 2/day.

1520.

A small village of woodsmen in this hex is engulfed in flames. The homes are built of timber and stone and surrounded by a deep moat and palisade (now burned to the ground). Ten malevolent mephits were unleashed on the village by a passing squadron of magic-users loyal to Princess Petal. The little demons have engulfed half the village and the surviving villagers (25 men, 60 women and 80 children) are hurriedly fighting the flames by passing buckets from the village's three wells. The village's largest building was its tavern, which is now completely aflame. Three of the poor souls that were trapped inside have already risen as spectres. They still stand at the bar drowning their sorrows in flaming punch.

Fire Mephit: HD 3; AC 3 [16]; Atk 2 claws (1d4); Move 12 (F18); Save 14; CL/XP 6/400; Special: Only harmed by +1 or better weapons, immune to fire, regenerate 2 hp/round in fire, breath fire (15-ft cone, 1d8 damage).

Spectre: HD 7; AC 2 [17]; Atk 1 spectral weapon or touch (1d8 + level drain); Move 15 (Fly 30); Save 9; CL/XP 9/1100; Special: Drain 2 levels with hit, immune to non-magical weapons.

1607.

This wide valley of fields and orchards is the location of Xom-Iforn, a large walled town famed as a center of learning and as the home of Farin, a master armorer known for his exquisite swords. The town is located in the middle of a lake populated by silvery fresh water eels and a delicious breed of giant crawdads both favored and feared throughout the Empire. The town's walls are gray and hoary and covered in vines of velvety gray flowers. The town is governed by a mayor elected by a council of guilds, making it the most progressive and dynamic settlement in the Empire. The guilds are dominated by the Brothers of the Hammer, the smiths' guild, with Farin serving as the power behind the lord mayor, Melot, a pompous windbag with more chins than sense. The town hall is typical for large buildings in the Empire – sloped walls, a flat roof ringed by iron spikes – but attached to it is a great bell tower in shape of the drunken god Galofin, Lord of Misrule. Galofin in the town's patron deity and his priests, garbed in gauzy, pastel robes sewn with silver bells, can be seen dancing day and night through the streets of the city singing ancient songs and collecting coins in their wide wicker baskets. The high priest of Galofin is Jacene, a troubled woman with a face that would be pretty if not marred by a crooked smile and wild eyes.

Jacene, Cleric Lvl 4: HP 16; AC 9 [10]; Save 12 (10 vs. paralysis and poison); CL/XP 4/120; Special: Banish undead, spells (2/1). Flail, holy symbol in the form of a silver bell cast in the visage of Galofin hanging from her silken cap.

1622.

Under a great pile of stones riddled with narrow tunnels there dwells an ancient wyrm called Mazhin of the Dappled Dome. Mazhin is a brilliant dragon, thoroughly wicked and contemptible, with a long body like a salamander and a six thin, bowed legs like those of a centipede. Its skin is mottled silver and titian and its eyes are large and as bright as flame. Mazhin has a taste for sentient creatures and the ensuing war has awakened him, for the smell of blood and fear taint the air. His lair lies in a little valley of amber trees and sparkling ponds speckled with transparent lilies and equally transparent frogs with poisonous hides. When adventurers enter this hex, there is a 3 in 6 chance that Mazhin will pick up their scent and investigate them. If not, it means he has gone further afield and is likely bringing back a captive, for he only devours his prey while sunning himself atop his pile of stones. His horde consists of 720 sp in a chest formed from a storm giant's skull (glazed electric blue and trapped with a 4 dice fire trap), 10,120 gp, a casket filled with 20 pounds of salt (worth 5 gp/lb), a small silver box containing 3 lb of chili powder from the far south (worth 300 gp/lb) and a brass icon of Murchuter (worth 400 gp).

Mazhin, Wyrm: HD 12 (96 hp); AC -2 [21]; Atk 1 bite (1d8), 2 claws (1d6); Move 9 (F30); Save 3; CL/XP 16/3200; Special: Breath a cone of fire (40 feet long, 20 feet wide at base), cast spells as 4th level magic-user.

1717.

Many of the villages of the Empire held charters of self-rule from the emperor. One such village, Priel by name, made the foolish decision to hire a band of mercenaries to bolster their company of militia. The mercenaries' captain, Hered, was a cruel looking fellow, with peaked eyebrows and a jutting jaw and under-bite. The man turned out to have a generous portion of hobgoblin blood in his veins and his mercenaries were full-blooded hobgoblins. Approaching the city in thick cloaks, the two companies of hobgoblins entered the village and soon took control. A day later, the men of the village attempted to eject them and were destroyed, their houses reduced to rubble and ashes, their women and children either clapped in irons or sacrificed to appease the warlike goddess of the hobgoblins, Calasa. The hobgoblins are now finishing plundering the village's meager treasures and stores and will soon head into the monster-infested hills south of the included map to sell their slaves and prepare for another campaign into the shattered empire. Of the original company of mercenaries, sixteen hobgoblins survive. The villagers once raised maize and apples and gathered wild thyme (which they used to flavor a fine gin) and the bark of the white willows in the hills surrounding the village, turning it into medicine.

Hered, Hobgoblin Chief: HD 5+5; AC 3 [16]; Atk 1 weapon (1d8); Move 9; Save 12; CL/XP 5/240; Special: None.

1719.

An injured man is hiding in the underbrush here. The man escaped from the hobgoblins that conquered Priel [1717] and six white apes are now hunting him. Random encounters in this hex are with the white apes. If the adventurers discover the man, there is a 10% chance each hour that the six white apes converge on them and attack. The man is a Northman with a severely injured leg (he has 1 hit point left and will die from infection in 1d6 days if not healed). A smith, he escaped a few days ago, leaving behind his wife and teenaged son but swearing to come back for them. The black sheep of a family that produced generations of loremasters, he knows of the Seven Sleepers [1510] and will share this knowledge with folk who free his family.

White Ape: HD 4; AC 6 [13]; Atk 2 claws (1d4); Move 15; Save 13; CL/XP 4/120; Special: None.

1802.

In the middle of this murky hex is a thick copse of swamp-apple trees. The trees have glossy, chocolate-brown bark, slim golden leaves and limbs that droop under the weight of their fruit. The apples are about the size of a large plum and look shriveled, with a brownish-tan skin and light pink flesh. Despite their unsavory appearance, they are delicious and a pound of the fruit is as good as a week of normal rations. The trees are inhabited by spindly monkeys with golden fur and violet faces. The monkeys are very aggressive in defending their trees and once per day are capable of growing to several times their normal size, becoming, in effect, the equivalent of white apes. Each tree is home to 1d6 of the odd primates.

Violet-Faced Monkey: HD 1d4; AC 4 [15]; Atk 1 bite (1d3); Move 12 (C12); Save 18; CL/XP B/5; Special: Transform into equivalent of white ape.

1811.

The drums of the war god Telos sound day and night in this fortress-temple situated beside a great lake stocked with giant bronze dragon bass. The temple is constructed of milky brown stone quarried in the surrounding hills. It is surrounded by an extensive orchard of thorny pear trees (the priests gather the pears and turn them into cider), the trees being sacred to Telos. The temple consists of an inner sanctum that contains the idol of Telos. The inner sanctum is surrounded by dormitories for the priests and visiting squires and other rooms common to a temple. Beyond the dormitories there are four large courts, unpaved and connected by arched gates with steel portcullises. Each court is fronted by a stone gatehouse, 30 feet tall with battlements and a gate of thick oak bound by steel. In each courtyard the walls are covered in friezes of the war god. The court of archers depicts him as an archer battling an army. The equine court depicts him as a horseman fighting a dragon. The court of swords depicts him as a swordsman surrounded by demons. The court of wrestlers depicts him as a wrestler battling three trolls. In all cases, Telos is depicted as a muscular man with bronzed skin, purple eyes and chestnut hair and beard worn in long ringlets. He is always depicted nude and carrying various weapons.

The priests of the temple are all retired fighting-men, some serving as lay brothers, others becoming clerics. The temple normally houses forty priests, aged 35 to 50 and all fighting-men of level 1d4+1. About 1 in 6 is also a cleric of level 1d3. All but five of the priests, the eldest priests, are now away at war, tending to the armies of Petal, Pearl and Peahen. These men and women take turns sounding the drums of war. They are accompanied by the high priestess of the temple, Xultenthe of the Auburn Locks. She remains behind to gather information on the campaigns as they unfold, the news brought by trained falcons.

The temple has a library of military literature and fighting manuals, of which they are justly proud. The temple's treasure consists of 2,650 sp, 2,690 gp and a rose quartz worth 2 gp and a bronze icon of Telos (worth 45 gp, dented where it was used to bludgeon a dragon to death). The treasure is kept in a hidden chamber and guarded by three separate poison gas traps – one causes sleep, the other erases one's memory and the other instant death.

Xultenthe, Cleric 10: HP 42; AC 4 [15]; Save 6 (4 vs. paralysis and poison); CL/XP 11/1700; Special: Banish undead, spells (3/3/3/3/3). Chainmail, shield, warhammer, holy symbol in the form of a cracked obsidian sphere on a chain and a brass torque worth 175 gp.

1815.

Among the various monopolies held by the imperial government, one of the most lucrative is that of almonds. None but the imperial authorities may grow almonds and only a very few well-connected traders are permitted to purchase them from the government and export them south and east. This hex holds the largest almond orchard in the empire. The orchard is surrounded by a twenty foot tall wall of mortared stone with battlements and a patrol of archers. A flight of five harpies has now taken up residence in the middle of the orchard. Having charmed and then devoured the guards, they now roost in the trees tending their blood red eggs.

1820.

Three will-o-the-wisps lurk in the forest here, bobbing about the ancient ruins of a stone cottage. The cottage was once home to a cunning man named Gavos the ruins are now overgrown with medicinal and mystic herbs. Should one take the time to clear the ruins, they may find a trapdoor that leads into the man's cellar, where sleeps a beautiful maiden, perhaps 13 years old, sunk in a golden vat (worth 1,000 gp) filled with airy water. An ominous, shadowy force is poised over the vat, ready to strike any who would free the girl, a clone of Gavos' dead wife. The shadowy force is Gavos, now a spectre.

Will-o-the-Wisp: HD 9 (48, 41, 38 hp); AC –8 [27]; Atk 1 shock (2d6); Move 18; Save 6; CL/XP 10/1400; Special: None.

Gavos, Spectre: HD 7 (30 hp); AC 2 [17]; Atk 1 spectral weapon or touch (1d8 + level drain); Move 15 (Fly 30); Save 9; CL/XP 9/1100; Special: Drain 2 levels with hit, immune to non-magical weapons.

2013.

On a broad meadow ringed by willows and stone monuments to past emperors and empresses, there stands the Hill of Kings. The hill, despite being spoken of in hushed tones of reverence and awe by most Northmen, is only 30 feet tall with a diameter that averages 60 feet. Atop the hill there is a granite platform, just large enough for a person to stand on, that is called the Crowning Stone for obvious reasons. It is here that a prince or princess ascends the hill bearing the Imperial Regalia and has the imperial key bestowed upon them by the High Priest of Talaunus, the God of Civilization.

The former Emperor Brodred did not trust his daughters and for this reason he mourned deeply the passing of his twin sons beyond the bounds of the empire and the knowledge of men. It is for this reason that he had the Imperial Regalia hidden beyond their reach in the possession of his guardian deva Tzaqiel [3822].

The hill is now surrounded by a dozen pavilions of imperial purple. These pavilions house the imperial guard, three squadrons of imperial knights (2+1 HD) and 6 companies of men-at-arms led by Cunovard, Constable of the Empire and confidant of Emperor Brodred. The men guard the hill and the stone, their faces blackened with ashes in mourning.

Cunovard, Paladin Lvl 9: HP 60; AC 3 [16]; Save 4; CL/XP 10/1400; Special: Lay on hands (18 hp), immune to disease, summon warhorse, dispel evil, detect evil. Platemail, battleaxe, dagger, belt buckle inlaid with sard (worth 500 gp).

2016.

Yal-Garok is the enormous center of the Empire, a prosperous city-state of 100,000 men and women, girded by colossal walls of blue-green stone and imposing towers patrolled not only by the best trained and equipped warriors in the Empire. It is in most respects a typical city-state of the Northmen, just on a larger scale. It is a walled and contains a myriad of buildings and towers, all with sloping outer walls and flat roofs ringed by iron spikes meant to discourage the invasion of the home by evil spirits. In fact, these spikes are a serious business in Yal-Garok and other Northmen towns, for they are manufactured by the different temples and sold to a superstitious public. Some of the spikes are enchanted with a *protection from evil, 10-ft radius* effect, but such spikes are expensive and rarely used even by the aristocracy. Yal-Garok contains the imperial palace, a castle of 200 rooms and 100-ft tall towers of the same blue-green stone as the city walls. The city-state also has four smaller citadels, each commanded by a castellan of the noble blood appointed by the reigning emperor and under the control of the Constable of the Empire, the supreme military commander. The current constable, Cunovard has left the city in protest of the war of succession, joining the imperial guard at the Hill of Kings [2013].

The streets of Yal-Garok are thronged with cautious merchants, spies, prostitutes of every shape and size, vendors of questionable viands, slinking guttersnipes, tricky charlatans, soldiers on leave, guardsmen on the take and endless processions of imperial nobles consisting of palanquins carried by teams of brawny servants and veiled by gauzy curtains. One can find nearly anything for sale in Yal-Garok, if not from a shop or street vendor then from the extensive "black market" that does business in the city-state's alleys and cellars. The city-state is especially known for its pastries, malmsey (a sweet, fortified wine), the beauty of its women, its towering temples (all the gods and goddesses of the Northmen are represented), especially the imposing pyramid of the sun god Vephus, and its manufacture of cloth-of-silver.

Yal-Garok is currently under the rule of Princess Petal, youngest daughter of the deceased Emperor Brodred. It was on her orders that one of the emperor's handmaids poisoned him with wild almonds. Within minutes of his untimely death, she and her personal guard had already moved to secure her power by seizing the Imperial Regalia, discovering to her shock and dismay that they were no longer in the imperial treasury. The princess' personal guard is composed of a squadron of amazons from the far south with skin like black marble and eyes of the purest blue. The amazons wear black, lacquered platemail and carry lantern shields (see New Weapons below) emblazoned with the pink rose of Princess Petal and daggers.

Princess Petal, Assassin Lvl 10: HP 53; AC 9 [10]; Save 6; CL/XP 9/1100; Special: Disguise, poison, backstab x2, climb walls 92%, delicate tasks 50%, hear sounds 5 in 6, hide in shadows 55%, move silently 60%, open locks 55%. Always keeps a poisoned dagger and a poisoned pin on her person at all times (save or die).

Amazon Guard: HD 2+1; AC 2 [17]; Atk 1 weapon (1d6+1); Move 9; Save 16; CL/XP 2/30; Special: None.

2019.

Tall, black elms in this hex are home to a flock of 1d10+10 harpies. The harpies look like a combination of carrion crow and white-skinned maiden and encounters with 1d4+4 of them occur on a roll of 1-3 on 1d6. Their lair lies at the center of the hex, which is strewn with bones, scraps of armor and abandoned weapons. There is a total of 1,200 gp worth of jewelry hidden in their foul nests.

Ravenous Harpy: HD 3; AC 7 [12]; Atk 2 talons (1d3) and weapon (1d6); Move 6 (Fly 18); Save 14; CL/XP 4/120; Special: Flight, siren-song.

2115.

Xom-Laoth is called the Black City of the East. Its name is derived from its walls, which are composed of black glass (an illusion – they are actually granite) while the towering castle in the middle of town is clad in white marble (not an illusion). The Baroness Catheryl rules Xom-Laoth with cunning and cruelty. Townsmen soon learn that it pays to be the baroness' friend lest they disappear in the night. The Baroness accomplishes this vanishing act with the help of a series of underground tunnels and a colony of goblins dwelling beneath the town that are absolutely cowed by the baroness. The baroness appears as a petite, almost fragile woman with ebony skin and a face that is loveliness incarnate. Her eyes are black and deep and her hair cascades down her shoulders like a silvery waterfall. It should be mentioned that the baroness is actually a succubus summoned and (partially) controlled by Princess Pearl.

Catheryl, Succubus: HD 6 (25 hp); AC 2 [17]; Atk 2 claws (1d6); Move 12 (F18); Save 11; CL/XP 12/2000; Special: Spells (charm monster, ESP, etherealness, polymorph, suggestion, teleport), summon vrock (30% chance of success), only harmed by +1 or better weapons, immune to electricity and poison, magic resistance (45%), telepathy 100 ft., tongues, level drain (must kiss victim).

2122.

You come across a line of prisoners in this hex, men, women and children, chained together and being lead to the White River by hobgoblin warriors. They will fetch a good price as slaves on the other side of the river, for the gnolls of the wooded mountains are lazy and will not sully themselves with labor when they can force another to work in their place. There are 50 prisoners, most in poor shape, and a company of hobgoblin warriors led by Budaur. Budaur wears a wreath of red carnations around his neck and a jeweled leather harness worth 400 gp. His sword is forged of the finest Xabian steel and bears the image of razorback hogs on the hilt and an impressive piece of glass (worthless) in the pommel. A ferret on a long silver chain is never far from the dandy hobgoblin, who despite his appearance is a fine warrior and a master tactician.

2202.

A shrine of green marble has been constructed in a grove of black willows. The shrine is about 12 feet tall and the interior measures 10-ft x 10-ft. The ceiling is a crossed vault, the floor paved with volcanic glass and on a dais in the middle of the room there is a bronze sculpture of a muscular man that has been stabbed through the back with a long sword. The man is balanced on one arm, his other reaching out as though for help. The sculpture has two amethysts for eyes (worth 300 gp each). The long sword in the idol's back can be removed; it is a *cursed -1 sword* that also imposes a -2 penalty on saving throws against demonic influence. When removed, the idol seems to melt into a bronze blob that then scurries after the intruders, intent on killing them.

Bronze Blob: HD 8 (40 hp); AC 1 [18]; Atk 1 pseudopod (1d6); Move 9 (C9); Save 8; CL 10/1400; Special: Immune to bludgeoning weapons, only harmed by +1 or better weapons, creatures killed by the beast begin to turn into black puddings from the inside out – the transformation takes 3 hours.

2205.

On a fertile plain as yet untouched by war there rise the walls of Xom-Coric, a town of 2,500 souls that now houses a mere 1,600 people, all women, children and old men. The rest of the men of Xom-Coric were pressed into service as soldiers of Princess Peahen and now languish in the slave pits of Princess Petal. The women and old men have had to take up arms against the goblin raids that have been occurring nightly since the warriors of the town were taken away.

2208.

Five hundred steps has been carved into the side of a gorge in this hex. Trickles of water run down either side of the stairs, streaking the black basalt with smears of green and rust red algae. At the bottom of the steps is Dancing Demon Gorge, named for the hundreds of basalt statues of dancing demons that stand amidst the maelstrom of white water rushing down the center of the chasm. The water ranges from 3 to 8 feet deep. The gorge is six miles long (i.e. it fits neatly in the hex) and the stairs are located near the southern entrance to the gorge. About one mile north of the entrance there is a tall statue of a particularly beautiful demoness holding a wand of ruby-colored crystal. Should one be foolish enough to reach for the wand, it disappears from the hand and appear in the hand of another at least 20 feet away.

The wand is a *wand of illusion*, and it will continue to vanish and reappear as long as one attempts to seize it using physical means. Worse yet, should someone fall in the rapids and perish (they suffer 1d8 points of damage each round from bludgeoning and must hold their breath to avoid drowning), their spirit rises from the white water and is drawn into the nearest demon statue, animating it as though it were a gargoyle.

Gargoyle: HD 4; AC 5 [14]; Atk 2 claws (1d3), 1 bite (1d4), 1 horn (1d6); Move 9 (Fly 15); Save 13; CL/XP 6/400; Special: Fly.

2314.

A smoking crater is all that is left of a town once under the sway of Princess Petal. It looks as though some titanic force reached down from the sky and lifted the entire town away, leaving only the crater and the moat (now more of a shelf) that surrounded it, along with some cast off timber and masonry and a field of corpses. While most of the corpses look to have died from arrow shot or spear, about 10% of them (and a majority near the moat/crater) show no signs of violence, are without their hair, have chins coated with blood and faces twisted into masks of horror. The crater is now inhabited by a beast summoned from planes unknown by Princess Pearl. The creature is a chlorine elemental. It looks more or less like a slower moving greenish-yellow air elemental and lurks close to the ground waiting for victims.

Chlorine Elemental: HD 12 (57 hp); AC 2 [17]; Atk 1 strike (3d6 + 1d6 acid); Move 6 (Swim 18); Save 3; CL/XP 12/2000; Special: Fumes as cloudkill spell in a 5-ft radius around monster.

2319.

The burned out remains of a roadhouse stands on the highway here. The roadhouse consisted of a two-story stone and wood structure with a walled courtyard (10-ft tall walls) and iron gate. The wooden portions of the house have been burned, but the stone walls and iron gate remain and the gate is locked. Inside the burned out structure one might hear loud voices. Following the voices leads to a trapdoor, which leads into wine cellar now occupied by seven swordsmen. The swordsmen have deserted their respective armies and found their way to this place. They now drink the dead innkeeper's wine and live off the food in his pantry, along with some hunting and trapping. All seven refuse to go back to war. Three of the men are deserters from the army of Princess Pearl and bear her blazonry of a white roundel on a black field. Three of the men betrayed Princess Petal and wear tunics bearing her pink rose. The final man deserted from Princess Peahen's artillery, as evidenced by his tools. He is an older man, with white hair and a heavy mustache. The deserter of Peahen, Ivarach by name, is actually a spy seeking information about the location of the imperial regalia. He knows 1d3 rumors.

Swordsman, Fighters Lvl 4: HP 4d8; AC 4 [15]; Save 11; CL/XP 4/120, Special: Multiple attacks, parry. Chainmail, shield, longsword, dagger.

Ivarach, Assassin Lvl 3: HP 22; AC 6 [13]; Save 13; CL/XP 2/30; Special: Disguise, poison, backstab x2, climb walls 85%, delicate tasks 15%, hear sounds 3 in 6, hide in shadows 10%, move silently 20%, open locks 10%. Leather armor, shield, hand axe, dagger, engineer's tools.

2407.

A rugged valley of grassy hills and shale and chert deposits lies in this hex, running east to west and crossed by a deep, lazy stream. The valley has a large village of miners set somewhat in the middle, the homes and businesses (blacksmith, three taverns, a foundry and a guild of caravan guards and bearers). The miners work several dozen iron mines burrowed into the surrounding hills, their presence marked by the resulting slag heaps. The miners and their wives lived here in relative peace, digging in the earth and raising sheep, sorghum, flax and delicious blackberries. Recently, they have received some unwelcome visitors, soldiers of Princess Petal, who have for all intents and purposes enslaved the people, putting them to work for a set price and shipping the iron back to Yal-Garok, the capital of the shattered empire to make weapons.

The soldiers have constructed a large, wooden fort in the center of the valley, overlooking the village. It has four 30-foot tall towers and 24-foot tall walls. Atop the hills that surround the ridge, the soldiers have constructed five observation platforms – 12-ft tall towers manned by 1d4+3 archers. The archers have bull's-eye lanterns that they use to signal the fort, which houses one company of men-at-arms and a squadron of horsemen of the famed Black Eagle Company, recognizable by their full black breeches, slit coats of mail, tall helms with black horsehair crests and round shields emblazoned with an eagle black on a field white. The commander of the Black Eagles, Pantiger the Kestrel, enjoys the sway he holds over the miners immensely and has become little more than a petty tyrant. Any intruders that enter the valley are seized as spies and put to work on a chain gang excavating a defensive moat around the fort. In order to keep the miners honest and diligent, the sixty women and children of the village have been seized and brought into the fort, living now in dormitories, the women being used to cook and clean for the soldiers.

Pantiger the Kestrel, Fighting-Man Lvl 7: HP 39; AC 2 [17]; Save 8; CL/XP 7/600, Special: Multiple attacks, parry. Platemail, shield, lance, horseman's axe (2d4 damage).

2410.

The valley that spreads out before you is crossed by two winding rivulets. Nestled in between those water courses are a patchwork of fields and dozens of pleasant hamlets. The farmers of the valley, called the Valley of Tulips, are as cunning as any and with the help of local scoundrel and libertine, Danucca, have held the forces of the princesses at bay – pledging their loyalty and produce to all three.

The largest building in the valley is the pyramidal temple of Almerla, the Goddess of Healing. The pyramid is surrounded by a grove of ancient hemlocks and the steps are planted with rows of tulips. Inside the temple there is an inner sanctum containing the goddess' idol, an inhumanly tall woman with an hourglass build, unclothed with porcelain skin and purple eyes, with an alligator curled around her feet. A dozen brass braziers hang from the ceiling on brass chains, burning a pleasant, narcotic substance that causes calm and sleep. The right eye of the alligator can be depressed, causing the idol to rotate to one side and revealing stairs into the deeper recesses of the temple.

Below the inner sanctum is a foyer containing a large basin of rose quartz filled with holy water. Low benches surround it, allowing priests to kneel and cleanse themselves. Clean robes of white edged with purple vines and flowers hang on pegs on the surrounding walls, which are made of white marble. One peg, turned counter-clockwise, opens a panel and leads into a series of living chambers and devotionary rooms that are brightly lit and hold turtle doves in pretty wooden cages. At the very bottom of the sub-temple there is a circular room, twenty feet in diameter and clad in serpentine. The mummified remains of nine lizardmen with long, crocodilian snouts line the walls of the chamber. They wear shrouds composed of lacquered black bronze scales and morning stars with long, nail-like spikes have been fitted to their hands. These spikes have been tipped with a sleeping poison – even a scratch sends one into a deep slumber of fitful dreams (saving throw to negate). These beings are the holy guardians of the temple, and can be called to action by any one of the priests by blowing on a pipes carved from the tusks of mastodons. These small pipes are worn around the neck on leather thongs.

Hidden in the depths of the temple is a treasure of 250 pp, 3,650 gp, a limestone idol of Almerla (worth 65 gp) and a large orange glass vessel filled with 10 pounds of mercury (worth 8 gp per pound).

Reptilian Mummies: HD6+4; AC 3 [16]; Atk 1 weapon (1d8 + poison); Move 9; Save 11; CL/XP 7/600; Special: Poisoned weapons cause sleep, only harmed by +1 or better weapons.

The high priestess of the temple is Xaathwen, a pudgy woman with wild hair and large hoop earrings of gold in her ears. She has gray-green eyes and a long, distinguished nose and carries a magic carpenter's hammer wherever she goes. While she does not entirely approve of the methods the farmers have used to keep the war from their valley, she is glad for it and will do nothing to spoil it.

Xaathwen, Cleric Lvl 9: HP 43; AC 4 [15]; Save 7 (5 vs. paralysis and poison); CL/XP 10/1400; Special: Banish undead, spells (3/3/3/2/2). Silvered scale armor, shield, carpenter's hammer (+1 club, +3 vs. undead, nails hammered into corpses protect them from undeath, hammered into the ground create a protection from evil 10' radius effect), holy symbol.

2412.

Xom-Velyn is a large town of unruly peasants growing fields of watercress in large ponds and keeping herds of goats. The town is a trading center ruled by a generous count called Rild. The town was the site of a historic battle between the founding emperor, Beroldern, and a red dragon. The defeat of the red dragon is one of the founding myths of the Empire, and it has made Xom-Velyn something of a pilgrimage site for the Northmen. A shrine of translucent yellow glass has been erected over the site of the dragon's slaying, the shrine resting in a field of poppies said to have been stained red by the dragon's blood. Each year, Count Rild holds a grand harvest festival that draws farmers, tradesmen, entertainers and thieves from across the Empire. Games of skill, jousting foremost among them, are held and honors are awarded. The town's treasury contains 180 gp, 460 sp and three platinum ingots hidden in the floor, painted to look like bricks. The ingots weigh 2 pounds each and are worth 100 gp each.

Rild: HD 5 (16 hp); AC 2 [17]; Atk 1 weapon (1d8); Move 12; Save12; CL/XP 5/240; Special: None. When prepared for battle, he wears platemail and carries shield and battleaxe.

2417.

Atop a hill bathed in sunlight (unless it is raining, in which case it is bathed in water) there are the ruins of a temple. Like most temples of the Northmen, it consists of a structure trapezoidal in profile – a flat-topped pyramid, so to speak, about 20 feet tall with wide stairs inlaid with precious stone on the north face. Atop the platform there is a veritable forest of columns spaced about 5 feet apart and covering the entire space except for a 10-ft x 10-ft space in the center of the platform where the idol is kept. The pillars are usually 10 to 15 feet tall and covered with a stone roof. The centermost pillars are twice as high and support a monolithic dome of some precious metal over a skeleton of iron and stone.

This particular ruin has lost its roof, the remains of which lie crumpled at the bottom of the hill as though a giant wind lifted it off and threw it. The dome and idol are nowhere to be seen and but a single column still rises from the platform, which is accessed via an opal stair (worth 5,000 gp if removed but to do so raises the ire of Sitric, the god of fire, to whom this temple was dedicated). The surviving column is fluted and clad in brass and bears images of fire nymphs in cloisonné. If one climbs to the top of the column, they discover a small niche filled with a transparent alien ooze that looks very much like water. If this creature is ingested, it causes wild hallucinations that have a cumulative 1% chance per hour of actually materializing in the real world (i.e. pink elephants might actually appear, forcing the Referee to roll a reaction check). The Referee should have the ingesting player recite a stream of consciousness of what he thinks he sees, with the Referee then secretly rolling d% to check if his hallucinations become reality about once per game hour. Each hour, the imbiber can attempt a saving throw to expel the alien ooze from his stomach by vomiting, at which point it slinks back to its "lair".

Alien Ooze: HD 1d4 (3 hp); AC 4 [15]; Atk None; Move 3; Save 18; CL/XP A/5; Special: Touch causes hallucinations (save to negate), immune to cold, fire, acid and electricity, resistance to bludgeoning weapons (50%).

2502.

This hex and the ones to the east and west are home to dozens of catoblepas and the weird swamp halflings that make their living off of them. The halflings milk the beasts, making a sour cheese that is not only favored as a spread by the Northmen but also provides proof against petrification. The halflings perform this feat by wearing leather helms that cover their eyes, relying on their trained noses and wondrous memories to find the beasts and draw out their milk. The halflings dwell in large, glass bubbles the color of golden honey that were discovered by them lodged in the moist ground. The bubbles were once used by the ancient serpent men to hatch their young, and are capable of housing 8 to 10 halflings comfortably.

Catoblepas: HD 6; AC 7 [12]; Atk 1 bite (1d6); Move 12; Save 11; CL/XP 8/800; Special: Lethal appearance.

2505.

This smoking valley is home to a massive seam of coal that has been worked for ages, supplying the cities of the Northmen with fuel for their ovens and forges. One branch of the seam has caught fire, making the ground uncomfortably hot and attracting three immature fire elementals and a gang of five smoke mephits. The mephits drove the miners out of the valley while two armies, in service to Princess Pearl and Princess Peahen, encamped on either side of the valley intending to seize it. Scouts from the two armies have had a few skirmishes, but otherwise relations have been fairly cordial, with opposing officers meeting often for dinners and

the men competing in a few rough and tumble games of harpastum, the national game of the Northmen. Each army is composed of 3 squadrons of horse and 4 companies of foot and commanded by a captain (HD 5). The army of Pearl is commanded by Gizur, while the army of Peahen is commanded by his cousin Colcot.

Fire Elementals: HD 4; AC 2[17]; Atk 1 strike (2d6); Move 12; Save 13; CL/XP 5/240; Special: Ignite materials.

Smoke Mephits: HD 3; AC 2 [17]; Atk 2 claws (1d3); Move 12 (F18); Save 14; CL/XP 6/400; Special: Breath weapon (cloud of choking smoke in 15-ft cone, 1d4 damage and blindness), regenerate 2 hp/round in smoky environment, only harmed by +1 or better weapons.

2522.

A caravan of dwarves is stuck here in the mire. The dwarves have traveled from their stronghold in the mountains to the southeast to sell arms and armor to the Northmen. The dwarves number eighteen warrior-smiths and thirty dwarf warriors armed with axes, mail, shield and crossbows. The dwarves travel in three large, odd conveyances that look like miniature arks standing on four elephantine legs. Gangplanks are used to mount and dismount the arks, each of which holds living quarters for the warrior-smiths (the common warriors sleep on deck), a supply closet and a small forge. The thane of the dwarves is Camril, a red-haired, black-eyed female with a muscular build and thin, sharp nose. Her consort is Hruairn, a more delicate dwarf woman with a square jaw and coarse, curly black hair and blue eyes. While Camril leads the smiths and warriors, Hruairn handles the business. As mentioned above, one of the arks has become stuck in a mire, and the dwarves are having a terrible time dislodging it. To make matters worse, two young green dragons have discovered the caravan and pick off its warriors nightly. Three men lie dead, their remains now rotting in the woods, the dwarves too frightened of the dragons to risk retrieving them. Camril is in a foul temper and has taken to calming herself with drink.

Camril, Dwarf Fighter Lvl 5: HP 40; AC 2 [17]; Save 10 (6 vs. magic); CL/XP 5/240, Special: Multiple attacks, parry, note features of stonework, darkvision 60 ft. Platemail, shield, warhammer, throwing hammer.

Hruairn, Dwarf Fighter/Thief Lvl 3/4: HP 10; AC 7 [12]; Save 12 (10 vs. devices, 8 vs. magic); CL/XP /60, Special: Multiple attacks, parry, back stab x2, climb walls 88%, delicate tasks 30%, hear sounds 4 in 6, hide in shadows 25%, move silently 35%, open locks 25%, read languages, read magic writings, note features of stonework. Leather armor, hand axe, two daggers, thieves' tools.

Green Dragons (2): HD 7 (21 hp); AC 2 [17]; Atk 2 claws (1d6), 1 bite (2d10); Move 9 (Fly 24); Save 9; CL/XP 9/1100; Special: Breathes poison gas.

2615.

A monastery of gray bricks, its walls shattered and stinking of brimstone, sits atop a gently sloping hill. The monastery contains a dozen chambers, including dormitories, a kitchen and a chapel, all in ruins. There is also a hall of wonders (all smashed) that contained a plethora of implements of civilization and learning. The hall contains a defaced idol of Talaunus, the god of civilization, that has been toppled and covered in dung that gives off an acrid odor that burns the eyes. Nine imps remain in the temple, torturing its six surviving priests in a cellar once used to hold foodstuffs and wine. The priests have been chained to the walls and they are routinely whipped.

The imps and the demon they serve were admitted to the temple by a wandering friar who chanced to meet Etheke [1118] the potion seller. The friar was consumed by the baalroch he brought into the temple. The demon, Shaalinsh by name (but not his true name, of course), descended into a grotto beneath the cellar and now reigns there over a court of twelve cultists drawn from the hills. The cultists have proclaimed him a god and bring him sacrifices in the form of fellow refugees that they capture in the wilderness. The new high priest has been endowed with the spellcasting ability of a 5th level cleric. The grotto houses a mineral spring, the walls of which are covered in red "pustules" that burst randomly (1 in 4 chance per round), spewing a sticky, acidic substance into the grotto. Anyone in the grotto during an explosion of goo must pass a saving throw or be struck for 1d4 points of acid damage, plus one point of damage per round thereafter until washed away. A person that suffers more than 10 points of this acid damage must save vs. poison or suffer frightening hallucinations (treat as *confusion*).

Imps: HD 2; AC 2 [17]; Atk 1 sting (1d4 + poison); Move 6 (Fly 16); Save 16; CL/XP 6/400; Special: Poison tail, polymorph, regenerate, immune to fire.

Baalroch: HD 9 (33 hp); AC 2 [17]; Atk 1 sword (1d12+2) and 1 whip (entangles); Move 6 (15 fly); Save 6; CL/XP 13/2300; Special: Magic Resistance (75%), surrounded by flame (3d6), magic weapon required to hit, unaffected by spells from casters lower than 6th level.

Cador, High Priest of Shaalinsh: HD 1 (5 hp); AC 9 [10]; Atk 1 weapon (1d6); Move 12; Save 17; CL/XP 3/60; Special: Cleric spells (2/2).

2708.

A band of hapless soldiers, survivors of a terrible battle that happened over a week ago, are desperately trying to defend an old fortified tower atop a craggy hill. They stumbled upon the tower one morning and decided to set up camp, allowing their horses some rest and their wounded time to heal. That night their sentries were attacked by a pack of 30 zombies raised by the inhabitants of the craggy hill. The zombies have kept the soldiers under siege for over a week, and their supplies are almost run out. The tower has a roof cistern that was filled by a recent rain, giving the men enough water to last two more days. The tower is three stories tall, with four-foot-thick walls and a sturdy iron door. The second and third stories have six arrow slits around the circumference of the tower, but the soldiers have found their bows almost useless against the zombies.

The aforementioned inhabitants of the hill are the aboriginal people of the country, elves with thin necks, pot bellies, long arms and legs, black skin and brilliant red hair. The elves have large eyes and long noses. They wear loincloths and leather bandoleers, being unaffected by the cold, and wield clubs and axes of polished wood and stone. The elves, who call themselves the Carudaa, raise crops of edible fungus and burrowing mammals beneath the ground, their halls lit by ghostly lights. The object of the Carudaa's veneration is a great turtle carved from a massive moss agate. They call this turtle Vuems and believe him guardian of the earth and creator of the Carudaa, he having scratched them from the rocks with his divine claws.

Soldiers (8): HD 1; AC 4 [15]; Atk 1 weapon (1d8); Move 12; Save 17; CL/XP 1/15; Special: None. Chainmail, shield, short sword, short bow.

Zombies (30): HD 2; HD 2; AC 8 [11] or with shield 7[12]; Atk 1 weapon or strike (1d8); Move 6; Save 16; CL/XP 2/30; Special: Immune to sleep and charm.

Carudaa: HD 1+1; AC 5 [14]; Atk 1 sword (1d8) or 2 arrows (1d6); Move 12; Save 17; CL/XP 1/15; Special: Immune to ghoul's paralysis, find secret doors.

2723.

An army of carrion orcs is on the march here. The orcs number 10 companies of foot and 4 mounted squadrons and are led by a hulking male with a lazy eye named Kaz the Impaler of Giants. The orcs have been hired by the Princess Petal, and one of her heralds, a scurrilous rogue named Rofnar, is riding with them. They are bound for Yal-Garok, but are undisciplined enough that forays into nearby settlements to plunder are likely.

Kaz the Impaler: HD 6; AC 5 [14]; Atk 1 spear (1d6+2); Move 9; Save 11; CL/XP 6/400; Special: None. Owns a +1 spear that drips with burning poison (save or 1d4 damage).

Rofnar, Assassin Lvl 3: HP 21; AC 6 [13]; Save 13; CL/XP 2/30; Special: Disguise, poison, backstab x2, climb walls 85%, delicate tasks 15%, hear sounds 3 in 6, hide in shadows 10%, move silently 20%, open locks 10%. Leather armor, shield, short sword, short bow.

2802.

A dolmen encrusted with sea salt stands in the middle of a rolling meadow occupied by dozens of wild goats. The goats wear copper bells that force creatures who hear them to pass a saving throw or flee the meadow. The dolmen is a portal that can be activated by passing through while whistling. Should one do this, they find themselves on an island in the midst of a vast, salty sea (actually, an intersection of the elemental planes of air and water).

The floating island is about one mile in diameter and is home to a spacious castle of multi-colored glass. The castle consists of a collection of geodesic domes, one sitting atop another forming a strange, lumpy pile. Each pane of glass on each dome is a different color, presenting a garish spectacle. The castle has no discernable entrance, but in fact can be entered through any of the panes of glass (which are as hard as steel) by a person holding a precious stone of the same general color (i.e. the holder of a ruby can walk through a red panel).

The castle is owned by an arch-wizard called Candle, a traveler through dimensions who recently took a sidewise step into a parallel world and stayed too long enjoying its exotic charms. When he reappeared in his own world, it was to discover the terrible war raging around him – a war he intends to remain out of. Candle is tall and thin, with a hollow-cheeked face, gray hair and gray eyes ringed by red (he suffers from terrible allergies). Although gentle in manner, he is fairly cold with others, forgetting names and taking an interest in people only so long as they are useful to him.

Candle keeps many wonders in his castle, including a large collection of glass unicorns (each filled with the blood of a mythic creature and having the powers of a random potion), an astral orrery constructed of precious stones and metals that moves on its own accord (each orb can be used as a *crystal ball* to see events on the planet it represents), visitors from many alternate planes and dimensions (the most recent being a green-skinned jungle amazon named Gundra), an enviable number of meads and wines and a 1956 Ford Fairlane in need of a tune-up. Candle's servants are a clan of 60 gnomes.

Candle keeps a treasure of 18,440 sp, 1,900 gp and a beryl necklace worth 7,000 gp in an adamant vault protected by an *arcane lock* as well as three mundane locks, each trapped with a poisoned needle.

Candle, Magic-User Lvl 12: HP 40; AC 9 [10]; Save 5 (3 vs. spells); CL/XP 13/2300; Special: Spells (4/4/4/4/4/1). Staff topped with bronze spheres, silver dagger, three darts, spellbook.

Gnome: HD 1d6; AC 6 [13]; Atk 1 weapon (1d6); Move 6; Save 18; CL/XP B/10; Special: Cast phantasmal force 1/day, immune to illusions.

2805.

The infamous scrutator of Princess Pearl, one Julion Pok, is on the hunt for the Imperial Regalia that will secure his princess' claim to the imperial throne. Julion is an ugly man with a face like a pinched ferret and gangly limbs that hint at a non-human heritage. His comrades, drawn from the retinue of his fiendish mistress, include the inscrutable Doctor Guthaire, a demonologist with one eye replaced by a yellowish opal, Rhuneda, a haughty young priest of Murchuter and the warrior twins Calla and Gunn.

Julion Pok, Thief Lvl 8: HP 24; AC 7 [12]; Save 9 (7 vs. devices); CL/XP 7/600; Special: Back stab x3, climb walls 92%, delicate tasks 50%, hear sounds 4 in 6, hide in shadows 40%, move silently 50%, open locks 40%, read languages, read magic writings. Leather armor, short sword, light crossbow, dagger, thieves' tools.

Doctor Guthaire, Magic-User Lvl 5: HP 19; AC 9 [10]; Save 11 (9 vs. spells); CL/XP 4/120; Special: Spells (4/2/1). Ivory-handled dagger, three darts, spellbook.

Rhuneda, Cleric Lvl 6: HP 21; AC 2 [17]; Save 10 (8 vs. paralysis and poison); CL/XP 7/600; Special: Banish undead, spells (2/2/1/1). Platemail (black, ornate), shield, light mace, holy symbol.

Calla, Fighting-Woman Lvl 6: HP 42; AC 5 [14]; Save 9; CL/XP 6/400, Special: Multiple attacks, parry. Ring armor, buckler, longbow, hand axe.

Gunn, Fighting-Man Lvl 6: HP 36; AC 5 [14]; Save 9; CL/XP 6/400, Special: Multiple attacks, parry. Chainmail, battle axe, throwing knives (4).

2812.

A squadron of cataphracts led by Sergeant Ottana, a striking woman with hair turned white from a scrape with a wight many years ago, is camped in this hex. Ottana is slender and well-muscled, with a heavy, plain face. She and her men-at-arms became separated from a column of Petal's army and are now working their way across the countryside completely lost, their scout having succumbed to the bite of a poisonous snake. Ottana is in a foul temper due to harassing attacks by goblins at night and rapidly dwindling supplies. She has an abiding hatred of her Princess due to a very public demotion from her captaincy over the palace guard, and would dearly like to get even.

Ottana, Fighting-Woman Lvl 5: HP 21; AC 2 [17]; Save 10 (9 with luckstone); CL/XP 5/240, Special: Multiple attacks, parry. Platemail, shield, longsword, throwing axe, luckstone (+1 to save and attack) of tiger's eye, worn on a charm around her neck.

2819.

As adventurers pick their way through a woodland path, they are presented with a wall of shadow. The wall is pitch black, intangible and cold to the touch. It runs from one side of the path to the other and stands about 12 feet tall. Should one attempt to walk around the wall, they discover that it follows them. Likewise, it increases in height if one attempts to go over it. As the wall grows and passes over vegetation, that vegetation is left dead – drained of vitality and stark white. Animal life that walks through the wall will find it to be 10 feet thick. Each round spent in contact with the wall drains one level (saving throw to regain that level after 1 hour) and inflicts 1d6 points of cold damage. The wall can be stretched up to 200 feet long and high.

The wall is a projection of an alien artifact, a probe of sorts, shaped vaguely like a 2-ft thick, 6-ft long spear and made of a pearly metal. The shadowy wall is a defensive screen projected by the object, which is half buried in the earth. The object was sent by a magic-using creature from a parallel dimension to gather information. That magic-user has found no way to send living matter through the veil between his dimension and that of this setting, which seems to vibrate at an unheard of frequency of 12.7 on the Yaldok-Gimdorf Scale. The object is, in essence, a sentient magical item. It is capable of floating a few feet off the ground and collecting and storing sensory data. It can communicate with a high-pitched, tinny voice that it projects into people's heads using their native tongue. The object lies about 50 feet beyond its defensive screen and can communicate with people beyond the screen if they make an attempt at first contact. If freed from its predicament, it happily joins a party of adventurers, offering its wit and wisdom at inopportune moments, projecting its screen if personally threatened (and only if personally threatened) and otherwise performing as few useful functions for the adventurers as possible. After one week, the object dematerializes and returns to its own dimension.

Alien Probe: HD 5 (20 hp); AC 3 [16]; Atk none; Move 12; Save 12; CL/XP 8/800; Special: Defensive wall, levitate, magic missile 3/day.

3014.

An army of Princess Petal is camped in this hex awaiting orders. The army numbers 3 squadrons of hobelars and 3 companies of militia armed with slings. The camp is surrounded by a shallow ditch and a fence of sharpened stakes and consists of dozens of white pavilions centered around the pavilion of the army's commander, Count Rence, a gentleman warrior of the old nobility sitting on orders to join the siege of Yal-Kirith. Tall and effete, Count Rence despises Petal and is secretly using his scouts to scour the countryside for news of the Imperial Regalia, which he would use for his own enthronement.

Count Rence: HD 5; AC 3 [16]; Atk 1 weapon (1d8); Move 12; Save 12; CL/XP 5/240; Special: None. Platemail, battleaxe, dagger, brass stud worn in his nose (worth 4 gp), tiger's eye on his helm worth 65 gp.

3022.

In a lighter part of the woods, dominated by elm and birch, there is a very unique garden. The garden consists of natural shrubs, herbs and flowers – anemones, bell flowers, buckeye, columbine, foxgloves, hemlock, mayapples, sarsaparilla and wild strawberry, among other things – beautifully arranged with stone monuments and dozens of human and humanoid skeletons. The skeletons are held together with wire and posed in many whimsical shapes. The architects and keepers of the garden are a circle of five treants of various shapes and sizes. The treants bear no particular ill will toward humanoids, but regard them as pests that they would rather not have in their garden.

Treant: HD 9; AC 2 [17]; Atk 2 strikes (3d6); Move 6; Save 6; CL/XP 9/1100; Special: Control trees.

3104.

This vast field looks as though it has been tilled by giants. In fact, it is a breeding ground for bulettes, also known as land sharks. The creatures burrow through the loose soil every spring, the males making intricate patterns around the females (male bulettes outnumber the females 4 to 1 usually), sparring when their patterns intersect. After the spring mating, the creatures head into the hills. Hunters from the area then converge on the burrows looking for shed scales and dead bulettes, though fights to the death are extremely rare. Creatures from deeper in the earth also come, looking to prey on the hunters.

Bulette: HD 9; AC −1 [20]; Atk 2 claws (2d6), 1 bite (3d12); Move 15 (Burrow 3); Save 6; CL/XP 11/1700; Special: Burrow.

3116.

A rocky mound in this hex is covered by creeping vines that bear putrid yellow flowers and a sort of black moss that is oily to the touch. A large boulder at the base of the hill is actually a secret door that swings easily when pushed from within. A tribe of 100 grimlocks dwells within the mound, emerging at night to hunt in the woods. They have recently found themselves in possession of no fewer than 20 human captives – refugees that lost their way. The grimlocks are led by a bulbous-headed mutant called Famiak, a creature with lank, slobbering jowls, upward jutting tusks, saucer eyes that radiate waves of psychic static and tremendous psychic powers. Famiak has long desired the Princess Pearl, and his soldiers roam the land looking for captives that might further his ends.

Grimlock: HD 2; AC 4 [15]; Atk 1 battleaxe (1d8); Move 12; Save 16; CL/XP 2/30; Special: Blindsight.

Famiak: HD 8; AC 4 [15]; Atk 2 clas (1d6); Move 12; Save 8; CL/XP 2/30; Special: Blindsight, psychic crush (save or suffer 1 point of damage equal to character's intelligence plus stunned for 1 round), ESP (at will), immune to fear.

3206.

In a basalt cliff face marked by patches of black cardamom, a crack has formed. The crack runs from about 10 feet below the top of the cliffs to the valley floor. Day and night, thin, yellowish smoke seeps from the crack, making the valley floor smell of sulfur. Nobody dwells in the valley, so nobody has yet discovered the crack – nor is it likely they would ever guess at its significance. Each day the fighting between the princesses continues, the crack widens just a tiny bit, until one day it shall burst open to allow the Acheronian warriors waiting behind it to pour into the world from the dark gulfs of space where now they dwell on iron satellites orbiting some far flung gas giant. The Acheronians appear as demonic men and women, with smooth peacock green skin, wide amaranthine eyes, bat-like faces with elegant fangs and graceful four-fingered hands and feet. The warriors wear hauberks of polished gorgon hide and tall, spiral helms and they carry a wide assortment of weapons forged from volcanic glass.

Acheronian: HD 2+2; AC 3 [16]; Atk 1 weapon (1d8+1); Move 12; Save 16; CL/XP 3/60; Special: Immune to fire and poison, berserk rage (+1 to hit and damage) when reduced to half hit points.

3208.

A gang of twenty flesh-eating zombies is beating the grasses of an overgrown field looking for an amulet dropped by their necromancer master, Vensterap the Veinous (you don't want to see him in short pants). Venestrap is currently lounging on his palanquin overseeing the operation, a cup of mead in one hand and a black lace fan in the other. Vensterap's zombies are armed with flails. The amulet they seek has the power to turn one's body into a rubbery substance. This rubber form allows one a certain amount of elasticity, though every extra foot they stretch their limbs reduces their effective strength by 2 points. They also suffer only minimum damage from bludgeoning weapons. The rubber effect can be invoked once per day and persists for 1 hour.

Vensterap, Magic-User Lvl 8: HP 28; AC 9 [10]; Save 8 (6 vs. spells); CL/XP 8/800; Special: Spells (4/3/3/2). Dagger, skull cap (made from a real skull), silver chain earrings (worth 15 gp each), black fan.

3210.

There is a recent battlefield located here in a hollow divided by a rushing spring and hemmed in by chalk embankments and tangled shrubs and trees. The battle was really more of a skirmish, and an ambush at that. A dozen bodies lie in and about the stream pierced by black-fletched flint arrows favored by the local goblins. Among the dead is a magic-user wearing a sleeveless robe of burgundy over a beige tunic and a floppy hat of black velvet. He grips in one hand a glass wand that fires cones of cold (4d6 points of damage) with but a single charge remaining. The surrounding foliage is kissed with frost and the stream is still half iced over from the battle. Any goblin corpses that might have been here were removed by their mates, who are still lurking in the wood. A company of these goblins are encountered in this hex on a roll of 1-4 on 1d6.

Goblins: HD 1d6 hp; AC 6 [13]; Atk 1 weapon (1d6); Move 9; Save 18; CL/XP B/10; Special: -1 to hit in sunlight.

3219.

Three male owlbears have made a lair for themselves in the barn of an abandoned farmstead located near the river. The farmers once raised cattle (driven into the wild, a few of them survive in the surrounding meadows and woodlands) and grew barley, rye and gherkins. The farmhouse was boarded up, but the owlbears have already burst in and consumed most of the stores in the place. They were unable to get into the cellar (it is accessed via a trapdoor) and it still holds two barrels of grain and a bushel of pickles. The owlbears resemble a cross between barn owls and black bears and are small for their species. They are excellent climbers, and might (2 in 6 chance) be found in the barn's loft.

Owlbears (2): HD 5+1 (37, 25 hp); AC 5[14]; Atk 2 claws (1d6), 1 bite (2d6); Move 12; Save 12; CL/XP 5/240; Special: hug for additional 2d8 if to-hit roll is 18+.

3313.

For century upon century the Northmen ruled their empire, working their fields and feeling as though they were the masters of the world. It cannot be stressed enough how deeply the war of succession has affected their sense of self, causing some Northmen to question their gods and others to cleave more tightly to them. Over one hundred pilgrims have now gathered in the smoldering fields of a town consumed by flame and toppled by engines of war. They have been drawn here by the exhortation of Sesnantus, a haggard old prophet of the ruined town of Xom-Malonar, once the jewel of the eastern empire, grown prosperous from trade with the Sea Lords that dwell across the green Aderumdoc Mountains.

Here, in the ruins of Xom-Malonar, Sesnantus proclaims the end of the world, when the great gods will extinguish the stars unless they are propitiated with the blood of willing sacrifices. Daily, five men and five women climb the top of the blackened walls of Xom-Malonar and leap to their deaths. Their blood is then drained into silver vessels that are paraded around the ruins three times while Sesnantus chants in tongues, until the vessels are finally marched into the center of town and their contents are poured into a deep well that Sesnantus calls the Womb of Dagor, the goddess of subterranean waters.

Of late, willing sacrifices have been harder to find, as pilgrims have set up their camp and began to re-establish Xom-Malonar and establish ties. Sesnantus has begun to drug his victims, relying on a corps of zealots to capture those out after dark. One hopes a band of hapless adventurers would not be so rudely treated.

Sesnantus has buried a small wooden chest containing 40 sp, 1,175 gp a spinal worth 2,000 gp and a porcelain candlestick worth 300 gp. The box is not terribly secure, and a poisonous fox snake (treat as viper) has crawled into the box and made a little lair for itself.

Sesnantus, Cleric Lvl 7: HP 41; AC 2 [17]; Save 9 (7 vs. paralysis and poison); CL/XP 8/800; Special: Banish undead, spells (2/2/2/1/1). Platemail, shield, light mace, holy symbol.

Zealots: HD 1; AC 7 [12]; Atk 1 weapon (1d8); Move 12; Save 17; CL/XP 2/30; Special: +2 to hit in berserk state.

3411.

The city-state of Yal-Kirith is besieged by the grand army of Princess Petal. Daily they hurl bolts and stones against its sturdy walls. Yal-Kirith is the city-state of Princess Pearl, and her banner still flies over its crumbling battlements. The tiles of porphyry and malachite that once clad the city-state's gate have been battered away by the assaulting army, revealing the pitted yellowish limestone underneath.

Yal-Kirith is situated in a land of rolling hills and thick copses of oak. A grand river flows near the city and once supported a lively traffic in barges and a steady shipbuilding industry. Those facilities have now been burned to the ground, their remains hiding sappers of Princess Petal, who are digging a tunnel that they will divert the river waters into to undermine Yal-Kirith's whitewashed walls.

The population of Yal-Kirith now numbers 14,000 people defended by the remains of Pearl's army. Starvation and disease have set in, but the proud princess refuses to give into her hated sister. Her army is commanded by General Vodach, an old warrior with a shard of silver dagger embedded in his temple (to remove it would mean certain death). Each night, her personal guard scours the city for virgins of age, imprisoning them in the dungeon that their mistress might seal a pact with a demonic power to deliver her city from its troubles. The city priests have been shut out of the citadel and they have received disturbing omens from the gods. One priest in particular, Mithyn, has taken to hiding young girls in the catacombs beneath his temple, which is dedicated to Waith, the goddess of death, in fear that the soldiers of Pearl seek them for ill ends.

The army encamped around Yal-Kirith ranges over the territory night and day seizing crops and livestock and seeking out potential attackers. Encounters with patrols of 2d6+6 men-at-arms occur on a roll of 1-3 on 1d6. These men are little better than brigands, and will not hesitate to attack a force they consider weaker than themselves. The besieging army is commanded by General Laira, a raven-haired woman who still bears the kiss of youth on her 40-year old face.

Princess Pearl's treasury holds 470 pp, 8,970 gp, 1,675 sp and a soapstone icon of Gorz'zt, her demonic patron.

General Laira, Fighting-Woman Lvl 9: HP 49; AC 2 [17]; Save 6; CL/XP 9/1100, Special: Multiple attacks, parry. Platemail, shield, spear +1, hand axe.

General Vodach, Fighting-Man Lvl 8: HP 39; AC 2 [17]; Save 7; CL/XP 8/800, Special: Multiple attacks, parry. Platemail, two-handed sword, dagger, jasper ring worth 85 gp.

Princess Pearl, Magic-User Lvl 7: HP 24; AC 9 [10]; Save 9 (7 vs. spells); CL/XP 7/600; Special: Spells (4/3/2/1). Wavy-bladed dagger inlaid with silver and set with a jet intaglio of a handsome horned devil, velvet robes, spellbook.

3415.

A tribe of big goblins occupies a hill fort here. The fort is composed of cyclopean stones – parts of an ancient ruin – atop a rocky bluff. The stones and the cliffs stand a total of 30 feet tall. The hill fort can be entered via a narrow set of stone stairs trapped with falling rocks (save or 2d6 points of damage). The interior of the ruin is now occupied by a dozen tents made of animal skins. The tribe consists of 15 companies of goblin foot and 3 squadrons of mounted goblins, along with their 180 females and 200 young. The ruins still have a crooked tower that is always manned by three guards armed with short bows. The chieftain, Krod, dwells in the tower with his "harem", a trio of ambitious female orcs named Bara, Gab and Raxa. The orc females fight as goblins, but they are far craftier. The goblins have warty, blue skins and lank bits of black hair that sprout in random spots all over their bodies. The goblins have a treasure of 220 pp, 4,400 gp and 4,120 sp stored in terracotta pots.

Goblin: HD 1; AC 6[13]; Atk 1 by weapon (1d6); Move 9; Save 17; CL/XP 1/15; Special: None.

Krod, Goblin Chieftain: HD 3 (8 hp); AC 6 [13]; Atk 1 by weapon (1d8); Move 9; Save 14; CL/XP 3/60; Special: None.

3416.

Two villages, veritable piles of stone huts and narrow lanes, are divided by the river here. The villages, called Vheeley and Vorsey, are a fine pair, with the men of Vheeley keeping excellent sheep and the men of Vorsey turning their wool into cloth and sending it downriver to be dyed and turned into clothing. Unfortunately, the industry of Vorsey is the more lucrative and the disparity in wealth between the two villages has long been a source of tension. This tension was only heightened when two rival armies (each consisting of two companies and one squadron), one of Princess Pearl, the other of Princess Petal, moved into the two villages. The river is now the front line on a small, cold war between the villages, egged on by the soldiers who are happy to allow the villagers to fight by proxy. Each day, two men come out to the center of the bridge and duel, the loser being tossed into the river to be fished out by the undertakers of the village, misters Galaw and Jaspasek, and prepared for a proper burial. The soldiers and villagers line the banks and sit on the slate roofs, drinking and hollering and rooting their side on. Minstrels work the crowds, singing madrigals and collecting coins and rumors.

Recently, the situation has become tenser by the disappearance of maidens in Vorsey and young men in Vheeley. Naturally, each side blames the other and the accusations threaten to become an all-out battle. The actual culprit is a hydradaemon, once imprisoned beneath the bridge and recently freed by the life force that has ebbed into the water as one man after another was tossed into the river to die.

Hydradaemon: HD 7; AC 0 [19]; Atk 2 claws (1d6), bite (2d6) or spit; Move 9 (S24, F12); Save 9; CL/XP 13/2300; Special: Spittle (5/day, 20-ft long, save vs. sleep), spells (cause fear, darkness, detect magic, dimension door), only harmed by silver weapons, immune to acid and poison, magic resistance (35%), summon 8 HD water elemental 1/day, telepathy 100 ft.

3503.

A small gap in the granite promontories that mark this hex allows one to enter a secluded valley. The gap is just wide enough to permit a line of people and horses and the trees and brush are so thick and unyielding that it might take a full day to finally purchase entrance to the valley. The promontories range from 150 to 300 feet in height and have steep, shear sides – climbing is certainly possible, but no easier than forcing one's way through the foliage.

The floor of the valley is concave, with a shallow lake at the center. One must travel about one half mile to reach the lake. A strange fortress stands at the center of the lake. The fortress consists of a stepped pyramid about 40 feet tall with an 80-foot tall tower rising from the top of the pyramid. Each of the tower's four sides bears the sculpted image of a goddess.

The winter goddess Thelti, ivory skinned with sapphire windows for eyes, looks to the north, the summer goddess Mirio, round and fecund with eyes of amber glass and areolas of rose-colored glass, looking out over the lake to the south, the spring goddess Bresa, wild and rangy with delicate fangs in her open mouth and eyes of orange glass, looks to the east and the matronly autumn goddess Scathno, with severe eyes of russet and robes of brown, gazes to the west.

Large stone platforms lead to the pyramid/fortress from the shore. Each platform is 8 feet in diameter and spaced about 8 feet from the next platform in line. They rise anywhere between one to four feet above the surface of the placid lake. The waters of the lake must not be touched or disturbed, for to do so awakens the spirits of the lake. Each turn, the spirits will do one of the following things to dissuade intruders …

1. Lower a stone platform into the lake to a depth of 20 ft.
2. Cause a stone platform to rise from the lake to a height of 60 ft.
3. Cause a platform to erupt in green flames (2d6 damage per round).
4. Rise from the lake in the form of **1d3 water elementals** (8 HD).

If the sanctity of the waters is maintained, one can walk across the platforms to the pyramid without challenge. The tower can only be entered via a secret door located 35 feet above on the upper thigh of the summer goddess. This door leads into a tunnel 40 feet long that ends in chamber A.

A – This circular chamber is occupied by the temple's first line of defense, five acolytes and their leader, Dubgal. All six are garbed in long, straight robes checked black and white. A leather collar studded with small opals (worth 10 gp total) rings each druid's neck and secures a black leather hood that covers the face. The druids wear leather armor under their robes and each wields two curved short swords.

Acolyte, Druid Lvl 3: HP 3d6; AC 7 [12]; Save 13 (11 vs. fire); CL/XP 3/60; Special: Spells (3/1), first mysteries. Leather armor, two short swords, holy symbol (leather collar).

Dubgal, Druid Lvl 8: HP 45; AC 7 [12]; Save 8 (6 vs. fire); CL/XP 9/1100; Special: Spells (4/3/2/1), first mysteries, shapechange, immune to fey charms. Leather armor, two short swords, holy symbol (the leather collar), brass key that opens the trapdoor in [G] below.

In the center of the room there is a spiral stair leading down. Four heavy chains spaced evenly around the room run from the floor to the ceiling, where they are held by large metal claws. If released from the ceiling, the spiral stair corkscrews upward to allow access through a circular panel in the ceiling.

B – Beyond the ceiling panel in A there is a ladder embedded in a marble wall. The ladder climbs 15 feet to a portal that leads into a circular passage clad in wooden panels. The passage is balanced upon what can only be described as giant ball bearings beneath it, and thus as one walks "down" the passage, it moves with them in the manner of a treadmill, the wood being separated from the stone and thus closing the entrance portal until one has caused the passage to move 360-degrees. The moving passage is so lightly balanced that only a dwarf or elf has a chance (1 in 12) of noticing the trickery outright.

At four points in the passage there are arches adorned with twelve highly polished and faceted glass hemispheres. Light falling on these hemispheres creates a strange prismatic creature that first appears almost like a pane of stained glass blocking the passage. These creatures have one hit dice per hemisphere (i.e. 12 initially) and cannot move more than 5 feet away from their arch. Their touch causes searing damage depending on the intensity of the light creating them – 1d4 for candles, 1d6 for torches and 1d8 for lanterns and *light* spells. They can only be damaged by destroying the hemispheres, with each hemisphere destroyed reducing their hit dice by one. Hitting a hemisphere requires one to hit an AC of 6 [13] and inflict at least 3 points of damage. Wooden weapons inflict half damage against the glass hemispheres. Attacks against the body of the creature's are useless, and wooden weapons used to attack them may burst into flames.

Should one reach the portal on the other side of the circular passage, they find another ladder leading up 10 feet to a trapdoor.

C – All of these temples have the same basic layout. The far wall is the interior of the sculpted goddess faces of the temple, the windows the sculpture's eyes. The eye-windows are located atop a low dais, which also holds a sacrificial altar of stone engraved with blood channels that direct liquid into a hole in the center of the altar surface. The ceilings of the temples are vaulted and 20 feet high.

C1 – This temple of Thelti the winter goddess is clad in white marble with sapphire-colored windows. The floors, walls and ceiling are clad in ice, icicles having formed on the ceiling above. A 2-ft thick pillar of stone in the center of the chamber seems to be the source of the intense cold, and chained to it is a large winter wolf. Combat in the winter temple is complicated by the ice on the floor and the icicles on the ceiling. Each round in which a person (but not the winter wolf) attacks and/or moves more than 5 feet they must roll 1d20 under their dexterity or fall prone and suffer 1d3 points of damage. This falling damage cannot reduce a character's hit points below 1. Whenever the winter wolf moves or attacks, the strain against the pillar causes some of the icicles on the ceiling to fall. Everyone in the room (including the winter wolf) is attacked as though by a 2 HD creature that deals 1d4 points of damage on a successful hit.

Winter Wolf: HD 5 (35 hp); AC 5 [14]; Atk 1 bite (1d6+1); Move 18; Save 12; CL/XP 6/400; Special: Breathes frost 1/turn (4d6 damage)

C2 – The temple of Bresa the spring goddess is clad in green marble and thick with long, slim vines hanging from the vaulted ceiling. The vines are strangle vines and there are six of them in all. Resting atop the altar (and ignored by the vines) is a unicorn. Hiding in small burrows carved into the walls is a clan of twelve grigs sworn to protect the unicorn and temple. The grigs avoid flying, for this brings them within range of the strangle vines. The unicorn ignores intruders unless attacked.

Strangle Vines: HD 4; AC 6 [13]; Atk 4 vines (1d6); Move 0; Save 13; CL/XP 6/400; Special: None.

Grigs: HD 1d4; AC 3 [16]; Atk 1 weapon (1d3); Move 9 (F15); Save 18 (16 vs. magic); CL/XP B/10; Special: Spells (entangle, invisibility (self), pyrotechnics and ventriloquism 3/day each)

Unicorn: HD 5 (35 hp); AC 2 [17]; Atk 2 hoofs (1d8), horn (1d8); Move 24; Save 12; CL/XP 6/400; Special: Double damage from charge, magic resistance (25%), teleport.

C3 – The temple of Mirio the summer goddess is clad in red tiles and hung with a number of round lenses of polished glass from bronze chains. Furnaces behind the walls keep the room quite warm. The dais at the back of the temple is home to an immature, though no less regal, dragonne. The lenses are enchanted to gather light brought into the room and emit it back at their source as a searing beam that deals damage as follows: 1d6 to the holder of a candle once every three rounds, 3d6 to the holder of a torch once every two rounds or 5d6 to the holder of a lantern or *light* spell every round. The lenses are attached to the walls and there is only a 5% chance of them retaining their enchantment if removed.

Young Dragonne: HD 5 (35 hp); AC 3 [16]; Atk 2 claws (1d4), bite (2d6); Move 18 (Fly 9); Save 12; CL/XP 6/400; Special: Roar (save or weakened, i.e. -1 to all attacks, for 1 turn).

C4 – The temple of Scathro the autumn goddess is clad in oiled wood the color of burnt umber. The smell of the oil is intoxicating and anyone spending more than 3 rounds in the room must make a save each subsequent round or suffer a -2 penalty to hit, save and to their Armor Class. Curled up on the dais is a giant serpent, thirty feet long and two to three feet thick.

Giant Serpent: HD 6 (42 hp); AC 5 [14]; Atk 1 bite (1d3),

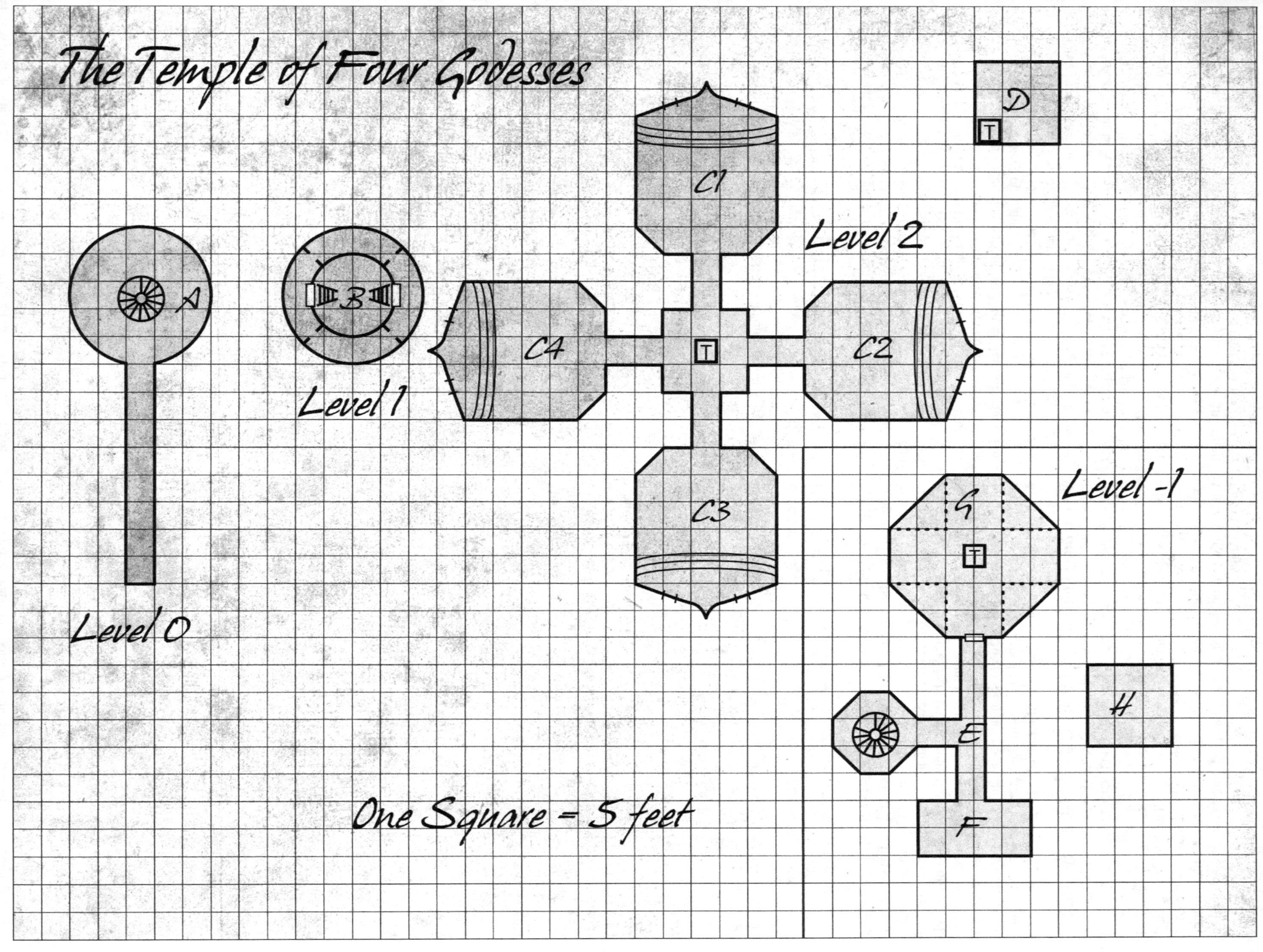

The Temple of Four Godesses
Level 0
Level 1
Level 2
Level -1
One Square = 5 feet
A
B
C1
C2
C3
C4
D
G
E
F
H

constrict (2d4); Move 10; Save 11; CL/XP 7/600; Special: Constrict.

D – The trapdoor to this chamber is located in the ceiling of the chamber between the temples. In truth, it does not exist until a ritual is performed, at which point the masonry simple disappears for 24 hours, allowing one to climb up (the ceiling is 10 feet high) into the secret chamber. The ritual involves killing the guardian animals in each temple and placing their bleeding corpses on each respective altar. When all four animals have been killed and their blood drank by the altars, the ritual is complete and the "trapdoor" disappears, leaving a 4-ft square hole in the ceiling.

The chamber above is clad in swirling, multi-colored marble that almost has a dizzying effect on viewers. In the center of the room there is a marble couch atop which relaxes the sculpted idol of a young demi-god, called Benthic by the druids of the temple. If he has not been summoned in chamber [F] below, Benthic appears here as a young, handsome man with a lithe, muscular physique. Benthic has the face of an angel, but merciless eyes and a single crooked horn jutting from the left side of his forehead. The idol is alive, inhabited by the spirit of the demi-god, who is child of the four goddesses. In his right hand he bears the famed *Scepter of Yal-Zanath*, one of the Imperial Regalia. The idol is sustained by the life force of the prisoners in the dungeon [G] below. For each of those prisoners rescued (see below), the living idol loses one Hit Dice.

Idol of Benthic: HD 10 (60 hp); AC -1 [20]; Atk 1 slam (2d6) or weapon; Move 15; Save 5; CL/XP 15/2900; Special: Only harmed by +1 or better weapon, will not be attacked by animals and plants, immune to elemental spells, magic resistance (50%), casts spells as an 8th level druid.

E – This long passage is cramped. The walls are covered with deep bas-reliefs of arms and legs that grasp at intruders. Each round, a person is attacked by 1d4 hands. The hands attack as 2 HD creatures and if they hit they hold the person and crush their limbs for 1d4 points of damage per round. The hands have an Armor Class of 5 [14] and are only broken if they sustain at least 7 points of damage from a single hit with a metal weapon.

F – This summoning chamber is clad in basalt that is carved into bestial, grimacing faces. Some of the faces have open mouths, from which pours sulfurous water that collects in a "moat" in the center of the room surrounding a raised platform. The platform is embossed with seals and glyphs that any druid, cleric or magic-user can tell are used for summoning a chthonic spirit. A large opal is set in the center of the platform and it is used by the demi-god in [D] above to collect energy from the prisoners in the dungeon [G]. Scattered around the chamber there are three jeweled brass braziers that emit an odorless red smoke. Each brazier is worth 50 gp. Tampering with the opal on the platform summons the chthonic form of Benthic (see D above). In this form, Benthic looks like a scaly gorilla with the head of a boar, leonine claws on hands and feet and a tail tipped with three serpentine heads like those of a hydra. As above, Benthic is sustained by the life force of the prisoners in the dungeon [G]. For each of those prisoners rescued (see below), he loses one Hit Dice.

Chthonic Benthic: HD 10 (60 hp); AC -1 [20]; Atk 2 claws (1d4), gore (1d6+2), 3 tail bites (1d3); Move 9; Save 4; CL/XP 11/1700; Special: Only harmed by +1 or better weapon, will not be attacked by elementals, immune to elemental spells, magic resistance (50%), casts spells as an 8th level evil cleric.

G – This octagonal dungeon houses six prisoners under the guard of four acolytes (as above). Five of the prisoners have had their eyes removed and replaced by opals. These three men and two women look drawn, their skin ashen, as though their life is ebbing away. In fact, their life energy is flowing into the demi-god Benthic (see D and F

above). If the opals are removed, Benthic is starved of power and the prisoners begin to heal, being completely restored in 4 weeks time. Each of the druids carries a brass key that opens one of the cells in this room. The trapdoor in this room blends in with the floor and is thus a secret door. It can only be released by inserting Dubgal's key (see [A] above) into a small hole in the northern wall. Similar keyholes are placed on the east and west walls, but tampering with them causes a sleeping gas to pour into the chamber (save or sleep, per spell).

H – A ladder leads down to the floor of this 15-ft tall chamber. The walls, ceiling and floor of the chamber are completely black. The room is filled with colored motes of light that swirl about the room. Should a mote come into contact with a person's head (make a saving throw each round to avoid this) it implants a memory in the person's head and steals away another, which becomes a different mote flying about the room. There are hundreds of motes, so the chance of a stolen memory being implanted in another adventurer (or re-implanted in the same adventurer) is only 1 in 300. Roll 1d6 to determine this new memory: 1 = Important information about the temple; 2-3 = A rumor about this region; 4-6 = A random piece of information made up by the Referee (4-6 on 1d6). The forgotten memory is as follows:

Roll	Memory Lost
1	One level's worth of training, including spells learned since that level was gained
2-4	Event from the past year
5-9	Event from the past week
10-14	Event from the past day
15-17	Name and identity of one comrade
18-19	Own family
20	Own name

3520.

The entirety of this wood is claimed by a clan of wood elves. The elves dwell in a luxurious tower that, to the eyes of mortals, blends seamlessly with the surrounding oaks (though the local treants and dryads think it's an eye sore and mock the elves relentlessly for their lack of taste and refinement). The top of the 5-story tower is an aerie where dwell six giant bald eagles, who deign to serve as mounts for the elves. The elves are defenders of liberty who have long been disgusted by the behavior of the Northmen and their empire. Several dozen refugees have been admitted into the elven wood (though not near the tower) and supported by the elven hunters. The tower houses 80 elven men and women and their seven spoiled children. Aemma and her elite squadron of eagle riders wear elven mail and carry spears, short swords and short bows. The other four companies of elves are practiced with longbow and longsword and wear leather armor.

Aemma, Elf Fighter/Magic-User Lvl 7/6: HP 21; AC 9 [10]; Save 8; CL/XP 8/800, Special: Multiple attacks, parry, spells (4/2/1), darkvision 60 ft., find secret door on 4 in 6, immune to paralysis from ghouls. Longsword, dagger, potion of heroism in a bottle hung around her neck, spellbook.

3610.

The northern market town of Xom-Krombak lies at the end of a highway paved with crushed granite. The highway leads into the mountainous peninsula north of the provided map, where dwell the Black Thinkers in their valley of crimson grasses and clay towers. The town has walls of ivory stone with sweeping battlements and tall, thin towers with burnished domes of green copper. Within the walls dwell 1,200 industrious men and women, who work the precious platinum pulled from the surrounding river stones. Xom-Krombak has no temples and no priests; giving the slightest utterance of a prayer or plea to the divine is cause for interment in one of the town's deep, black pits of correction. The pits are placed throughout the town and are in fact bricked sinkholes that lead into a maze of limestone caverns, all of which lead eventually to the prison of the red dragon Neach, whose breath stokes the fires of the town's great foundry (for it is said that only the breath of dragons is hot enough to melt platinum).

The foundry is a conical brick building that belches smoke day and night. Dwarves invited from their strongholds in the Adurumdoc Mountains swarm about the building like bees in a hive, processing their platinum and forming it into ingots for shipment to the chartered platinum smiths of the town. So important is the foundry, that it is completely surrounded by Xom-Krombak's citadel, itself a massive shell keep six stories tall. The keep has ivory walls that mimic the walls of the town, with sloped inner roofs of amber glass and magnificent hanging gardens worked by dozens of halfling slaves imported from the far west. The lord of the town and citadel is Sir Brothian, a knight with a bland, square face. For all his puissance at arms, Brothian is a naïve fool, more comfortable with soldiers and military campaigns than with women, especially his lady wife, the fair Isorwes. Isorwes is presently enjoying his absence fighting in the service of the Princess Pearl, having taken several young lovers in a bid to consolidate her power over the remaining men-at-arms.

The town treasury contains 2,780 gp, a copper dish worth 950 gp and a bronze brazier worth 165 gp.

Sir Brothian, Fighting-Man Lvl 11: HP 66; AC 2 [17]; Save 4; CL/XP 11/1700, Special: Multiple attacks, parry. Platemail, battleaxe, dagger, silver inlaid great helm worth 3,000 gp.

Neach: HD 13 (65 hp); AC 2 [17]; Atk 1 bite (2d6); Move 12 (F24); Save 3; CL/XP 15/2900; Special: Breath weapon 3/day (cone of fire 30-ft long and 15-ft wide at base)

3613.

A band of 20 brigands, deserters from an army of Princess Peahen, have set up a camp here in a copse of white oaks. They have constructed sleeping platforms in the trees and buried their loot (70 cp, 600 sp, 200 gp and a moonstone worth 135 gp) in three separate locations in the copse. Bow armed guards are always on the lookout day and night for intruders and they do not wait to ask for one's identity or loyalty before they attack, for the brigands know to announce themselves with the hoot of a night owl before approaching the camp. There are 30 bandits in all, wearing ring armor and carrying light crossbows, spears and daggers. Their leader is a charismatic sergeant-at-arms called Bogsby, a gruff blowhard who, truth be told, is little more than a fat poser using his men to avoid making an honest living. He fancies himself the captain of a free company and he is willing to sell his soldiers' services to adventurers, though once treasure comes into the picture it is a guarantee the "mercenaries" will turn on their employers.

Captain Bogsby: HD 3 (13 hp); AC 8 [13]; Atk 1 weapon (1d8); Move 12; Save 17; CL/XP 3/60; Special: None.

Brigand: HD 1; AC 7 [12]; Atk 1 weapon (1d8); Move 12; Save 17; CL/XP 1/15; Special: None.

3707.

Twelve ogre mercenaries are making their way into the thick of the human war in search of plunder and/or employment. The creatures bear giant axes and spears and, in one case, a small cannon (treat as 3 dice *fireball* that can be fired once every 4 rounds). The ogres possess 640 sp and 1,800 gp in treasure, as well as a generous supply of fresh venison (treat as 7 days of normal rations).

Ogre: HD 4+1; AC 5[14]; Atk 1 weapon (1d10+1); Move 9; Save 13; CL/XP 4/120; Special: None.

3717.

An odd automaton is cutting a path through the woodlands here. The war engine appears to be a crystal globe balanced upon four spindly metal legs. Rising from the top of the sphere is a metal pole to which are attached three chains tipped by rather large metal spheres. The spheres rotate about the pole, destroying everything in their path. Inside the sphere there is a terrified youth whose clothing suggests that he is an apprentice magic-user. The young man is unaware that the machine is driven by emotion and his desperation to free himself (the sphere is actually a sphere of force that disappears when the user wills it to disappear while in a state of calm) has caused the machine to go berserk. The machine is the creation of the wizard Vlick, arms-master of Princess Pearl and recently lost to an assassin's bolt while preparing to march to war in his creation. The sphere of force can be dispelled, but cannot be harmed in any other way.

War Machine: HD 10; AC 2 [17]; Atk 8 machine gun shots (2d6), mortar (4d6); Move 12; Save 3; CL/XP 13/2300; Special: None.

Kiran, Magic-User Lvl 1: HP 5; AC 9 [10]; Save 15 (13 vs. spells); CL/XP B/10; Special: Spells (1). Dagger, spellbook (left behind).

3811.

A tapestry has been rolled up and stuffed in a hollow oak tree here. The tapestry depicts Bresa, the wild spring goddess of the Northmen, plucking a silver harp while surrounded by a pack of baying wolves. Under a full moon, one can reach into the tapestry and pull out the harp. The harp can be used to summon a pack of 1d3+4 wolves when played under a waxing moon at night.

3819.

A caravan from the eastern shore, the land of the Sea Lords, has wound its way through the steep valleys of the Aderumdoc Mountains, ostensibly to trade with the Northmen, but really to scout for a large army gathering on the other side of the mountains. The caravan consists of ten traders and three squadrons of men-at-arms, one of mounted crossbowmen and two of light cavalry. The men of the Sea Lordies are exceptionally tall, with high-bridged noses, pale skin, hair that ranges from blonde to auburn in color and close set eyes of blue or gray. They wear leather tricorne hats, padded doublets and baggy pants tucked into tasseled buskins. Each of the traders is really a sergeant-at-arms of a hobelar squadron and leads a warhorse loaded with bundles of tobacco and exotic spices from the coast (each horse carries 300 gp worth of each). The assemblage is commanded by Captain Vilbran, a kindly man in a yellow jack-of-plates (treat as ring armor) with three cockatoo feathers stuck into his hat. The traders are interested in any news of the war of succession that they can gather.

Captain Vilbran, Fighting-Man Lvl 5: HP 32; AC 7 [12]; Save 10; CL/XP 5/240, Special: Multiple attacks, parry. Leather armor, longsword, throwing axe, light crossbow.

3822.

A 30-ft tall marble pillar surmounted by a golden statue (worth 10,000 XP, but weighs 750 lb) of the recently deceased Emperor Brodred has been placed here by unknown hands. Hidden by tall oaks, it has not yet been discovered by others. The pillar sits upon a marble platform 6 feet in diameter and about 2 feet tall. At the bottom of the pillar, the platform forms a small basin. Should a person fill this small basin with holy water (it takes one gallon) while placing his hands on the pillar and praying to a lawful deity, the surrounding countryside fades away and is replaced with a vast starscape, the stars actually being countless devas orbiting the pillar at a great distance. In due time, one deva approaches the pillar and platform. This deva is called Tzaqiel and was assigned to protect the Emperor Brodred by the celestial bureaucracy. Tzaqiel is aware that the emperor was poisoned by the hand of the Princess Petal and will charge the person who entered this pocket dimension with a *quest* to see her brought to justice. Tzaqiel is in possession of the *Crown of Yal-Garok*, but will only hand it over to a person who can defeat him in combat.

Tzaqiel: HD 10 (70 hp); AC -2 [21]; Atk 2 weapons (3d6); Move 18 (F36); Save 5; CL/XP 18/3500; Special: Wields two maces +3/+5 vs. constructed creatures, immune to acid, cold and death effects, resistance to electricity and fire (50%), spells – charm elemental (per charm monster, but only affects elementals), continual light, cure disease, cure light wounds (7/day), detect evil, dispel magic, hold monster (1/day), holy word, invisibility (self only), mirror image (7/day), polymorph self and remove curse.

New Weapons

Lantern Shield: This strange weapon is a buckler attached to a spiked gauntlet and a longsword. The buckler is itself spiked and it has a hook to which a lantern can be attached. The lantern shield provides a -1 [+1] bonus to Armor Class or can be used as a weapon that deals 1d6+1 points of damage.

New Monsters

Mastodon
Hit Dice: 13
Armor Class: 6 [13]
Attack: Gore (2d8)
Saving Throw: 3
Special: Trample
Move: 12
Alignment: Neutrality
Challenge Level/XP: 13/60

Mastodons are woolly relatives of the elephant common to the steppes and savannahs. Their tusks sometimes extend up to 10 feet in length. The Northmen use them as living engines of war, much as the Carthaginians used elephants.

Centaurs as a Playable Race

A centaur has the head, arms and torso of a human or elf and the lower body of a pony or ass. Centaurs dwell in meadows and glades surrounded by thick woodlands. They are known for their lack of temper and their fondness for women, war and song.

Centaurs are usually seven to eight feet tall from hoof to head. Even though their equine bodies are smaller than normal horses, they are still quite heavy and find it difficult to scale sheer surfaces without help from others. A centaur's equine body may have any pattern common to normal horses, and the hair on their heads often follows suit. Centaurs usually have nut brown skin.

Centaurs speak their own language and often (50%) the language of elves. They occasionally speak the common tongue of men. Many centaurs learn the languages of gnomes, goblins, halflings, kobolds and orcs. Because of their size, centaurs have booming voices.

Centaurs cannot have a strength or constitution scores lower than 9, nor can they have a wisdom score higher than 14. Centaurs can become fighting-men, advancing to a maximum of 7th level (8th level if strength is 14 or higher, 9th level if strength is 18). Centaurs can carry 150% more than most characters. In addition, their base movement is increased by 6. Because they are quadrupeds, a centaur's gets a +2 save to avoid being knocked over or grappled. In combat, centaurs can choose to attack with their weapon or their hooves, which deal 1d4 points of damage. A centaur's armor (really a combination of human armor and horse barding) costs twice as much as normal human armor.

Hex Crawl Chronicles: The Shattered Empire is written under version 1.0a of the Open Game License. As of yet, none of the material first appearing in **Hex Crawl Chronicles: The Shattered Empire** is considered Open Game Content.

OPEN GAME LICENSE Version 1.0a

The following text is the property of Wizards of the Coast, Inc. and is Copyright 2000 Wizards of the Coast, Inc ("Wizards"). All Rights Reserved.

1. Definitions: (a)"Contributors" means the copyright and/or trademark owners who have contributed Open Game Content; (b)"Derivative Material" means copyrighted material including derivative works and translations (including into other computer languages), potation, modification, correction, addition, extension, upgrade, improvement, compilation, abridgment or other form in which an existing work may be recast, transformed or adapted; (c) "Distribute" means to reproduce, license, rent, lease, sell, broadcast, publicly display, transmit or otherwise distribute; (d)"Open Game Content" means the game mechanic and includes the methods, procedures, processes and routines to the extent such content does not embody the Product Identity and is an enhancement over the prior art and any additional content clearly identified as Open Game Content by the Contributor, and means any work covered by this License, including translations and derivative works under copyright law, but specifically excludes Product Identity. (e) "Product Identity" means product and product line names, logos and identifying marks including trade dress; artifacts; creatures characters; stories, storylines, plots, thematic elements, dialogue, incidents, language, artwork, symbols, designs, depictions, likenesses, formats, poses, concepts, themes and graphic, photographic and other visual or audio representations; names and descriptions of characters, spells, enchantments, personalities, teams, personas, likenesses and special abilities; places, locations, environments, creatures, equipment, magical or supernatural abilities or effects, logos, symbols, or graphic designs; and any other trademark or registered trademark clearly identified as Product identity by the owner of the Product Identity, and which specifically excludes the Open Game Content; (f) "Trademark" means the logos, names, mark, sign, motto, designs that are used by a Contributor to identify itself or its products or the associated products contributed to the Open Game License by the Contributor (g) "Use", "Used" or "Using" means to use, Distribute, copy, edit, format, modify, translate and otherwise create Derivative Material of Open Game Content. (h) "You" or "Your" means the licensee in terms of this agreement.

2. The License: This License applies to any Open Game Content that contains a notice indicating that the Open Game Content may only be Used under and in terms of this License. You must affix such a notice to any Open Game Content that you Use. No terms may be added to or subtracted from this License except as described by the License itself. No other terms or conditions may be applied to any Open Game Content distributed using this License.

3.Offer and Acceptance: By Using the Open Game Content You indicate Your acceptance of the terms of this License.

4. Grant and Consideration: In consideration for agreeing to use this License, the Contributors grant You a perpetual, worldwide, royalty-free, non-exclusive license with the exact terms of this License to Use, the Open Game Content.

5.Representation of Authority to Contribute: If You are contributing original material as Open Game Content, You represent that Your Contributions are Your original creation and/or You have sufficient rights to grant the rights conveyed by this License.

6.Notice of License Copyright: You must update the COPYRIGHT NOTICE portion of this License to include the exact text of the COPYRIGHT NOTICE of any Open Game Content You are copying, modifying or distributing, and You must add the title, the copyright date, and the copyright holder's name to the COPYRIGHT NOTICE of any original Open Game Content you Distribute.

7. Use of Product Identity: You agree not to Use any Product Identity, including as an indication as to compatibility, except as expressly licensed in another, independent Agreement with the owner of each element of that Product Identity. You agree not to indicate compatibility or co-adaptability with any Trademark or Registered Trademark in conjunction with a work containing Open Game Content except as expressly licensed in another, independent Agreement with the owner of such Trademark or Registered Trademark. The use of any Product Identity in Open Game Content does not constitute a challenge to the ownership of that Product Identity. The owner of any Product Identity used in Open Game Content shall retain all rights, title and interest in and to that Product Identity.

8. Identification: If you distribute Open Game Content You must clearly indicate which portions of the work that you are distributing are Open Game Content.

9. Updating the License: Wizards or its designated Agents may publish updated versions of this License. You may use any authorized version of this License to copy, modify and distribute any Open Game Content originally distributed under any version of this License.

10. Copy of this License: You MUST include a copy of this License with every copy of the Open Game Content You Distribute.

11. Use of Contributor Credits: You may not market or advertise the Open Game Content using the name of any Contributor unless You have written permission from the Contributor to do so.

12. Inability to Comply: If it is impossible for You to comply with any of the terms of this License with respect to some or all of the Open Game Content due to statute, judicial order, or governmental regulation then You may not Use any Open Game Material so affected.

13. Termination: This License will terminate automatically if You fail to comply with all terms herein and fail to cure such breach within 30 days of becoming aware of the breach. All sublicenses shall survive the termination of this License.

14. Reformation: If any provision of this License is held to be unenforceable, such provision shall be reformed only to the extent necessary to make it enforceable.

15. COPYRIGHT NOTICE

Open Game License v 1.0a Copyright 2000, Wizards of the Coast, Inc.

System Reference Document Copyright 2000-2003, Wizards of the Coast, Inc.; Authors Jonathan Tweet, Monte Cook, Skip Williams, Rich Baker, Andy Collins, David Noonan, Rich Redman, Bruce R. Cordell, John D. Rateliff, Thomas Reid, James Wyatt, based on original material by E. Gary Gygax and Dave Arneson.

Swords & Wizardry Core Rules, Copyright 2008, Matthew J. Finch

Monster Compendium: 0e, Copyright 2008, Matthew J. Finch

Sword & Wizardry Complete Rules, Copyright, 2010, Matthew J. Finch

Angel, Monadic Deva, from the *Tome of Horrors Complete,* Copyright 2011, Necromancer Games, Inc., published and distributed by Frog God Games; Author Scott Greene, based on original material by Gary Gygax.

Angel, Movanic Deva , from the *Tome of Horrors Complete,* Copyright 2011, Necromancer Games, Inc., published and distributed by Frog God Games; Author Scott Greene, based on original material by Gary Gygax

Atomie, from the *Tome of Horrors Complete,* Copyright 2011, Necromancer Games, Inc., published and distributed by Frog God Games; Author Scott Greene, based on original material by Gary Gygax.

Daemon, Guardian, from the *Tome of Horrors Complete,* Copyright 2011, Necromancer Games, Inc., published and distributed by Frog God Games; Author Scott Greene, based on original material by Ian McDowall.

Daemon, Hydra, from the *Tome of Horrors Complete,* Copyright 2011, Necromancer Games, Inc., published and distributed by Frog God Games; Author Scott Greene, based on original material by Gary Gygax.

Rat, Shadow, from the *Tome of Horrors Complete,* Copyright 2011, Necromancer Games, Inc., published and distributed by Frog God Games; Authors Clark Peterson and Scott Greene.

Modern System Reference Document Copyright 2002-2004, Wizards of the Coast, Inc.; Authors Bill Slavicsek, Jeff Grubb, Rich Redman, Charles Ryan, Eric Cagle, David Noonan, Stan!, Christopher Perkins, Rodney Thompson, and JD Wiker, based on material by Jonathan Tweet, Monte Cook, Skip Williams, Richard Baker, Peter Adkison, Bruce R. Cordell, John Tynes, Andy Collins, and JD Wiker.

Castles & Crusades: Players Handbook, Copyright 2004, Troll Lord Games; Authors Davis Chenault and Mac Golden.

Cave Cricket from the Tome of Horrors, copyright 2002, Necromancer Games, Inc.; Authors Scott Greene and Clark Peterson, based on original material by Gary Gygax.

Crab, Monstrous from the Tome of Horrors, copyright 2002, Necromancer Games, Inc.; Author Scott Greene, based on original material by Gary Gygax.

Fly, Giant from the Tome of Horrors, copyright 2002, Necromancer Games, Inc.; Author Scott Greene, based on original material by Gary Gygax.

Golem, Wood from the Tome of Horrors, copyright 2002, Necromancer Games, Inc.; Authors Scott Greene and Patrick Lawinger.

Kamadan from the Tome of Horrors, copyright 2002, Necromancer Games, Inc.; Author Scott Greene, based on original material by Nick Louth.

Rot Grub from the Tome of Horrors, Copyright 2002, Necromancer Games, Inc.; Authors Scott Greene and Clark Peterson, based on original material by Gary Gygax

*Labyrinth Lord*TM Copyright 2007-2009, Daniel Proctor. Author Daniel Proctor.

Hex Crawl Chronicles: The Shattered Empire, Copyright 2012, Author John Stater.

www.ingramcontent.com/pod-product-compliance
Lightning Source LLC
Chambersburg PA
CBHW081329090726
47907CB00010B/2421